Showdown

Pyle turned to Dawson and pointed at the lawman. "Why, that's Gideon Hawk."

"Shut up, Beaver Face," said Lucius Running Bear, peeling his lips back from his gritted teeth and regarding Gideon Hawk, flinty-eyed, his big chest rising and falling sharply.

"Don't do anything stupid," Hawk said slowly, inching his left hand down toward the stag-butted Army Colt on his hip. "Just tell me where you last saw Ned."

Ken Dawson stepped back slowly, his breathing growing erratic. "Where we last seen Ned?" he stalled.

"Yeah, that's right."

Running Bear stood where he was, but Pyle skitter-stepped sideways and back, his face flushing so red that the whites of his eyes stood out like pearls. He was breathing hard, his hands leaving sweat streaks on his Spencer carbine.

His gaze raking them, seeing what was coming, Hawk said softly, "Don't do it."

He'd barely got the last word out when Beaver Face dropped his Spencer's barrel, thumbing the hammer back.

The rifle swung toward Hawk.

ROGUE LAWMAN

Peter Brandvold

BERKLEY BOOKS, NEW YORK

THE BERKLEY PUBLISHING GROUP
Published by the Penguin Group
Penguin Group (USA) Inc.
375 Hudson Street, New York, New York 10014, USA
Penguin Group (Canada), 90 Eglinton Avenue East, Suite 700, Toronto, Ontario M4P 2Y3, Canada
(a division of Pearson Penguin Canada Inc.)
Penguin Books Ltd., 80 Strand, London WC2R 0RL, England
Penguin Group Ireland, 25 St. Stephen's Green, Dublin 2, Ireland (a division of Penguin Books Ltd.)
Penguin Group (Australia), 250 Camberwell Road, Camberwell, Victoria 3124, Australia
(a division of Pearson Australia Group Pty. Ltd.)
Penguin Books India Pvt. Ltd., 11 Community Centre, Panchsheel Park, New Delhi—110 017, India
Penguin Group (NZ), Cnr. Airborne and Rosedale Roads, Albany, Auckland 1310, New Zealand
(a division of Pearson New Zealand Ltd.)
Penguin Books (South Africa) (Pty.) Ltd., 24 Sturdee Avenue, Rosebank, Johannesburg 2196,
South Africa

Penguin Books Ltd., Registered Offices: 80 Strand, London WC2R 0RL, England

This is a work of fiction. Names, characters, places, and incidents either are the product of the author's imagination or are used fictitiously, and any resemblance to actual persons, living or dead, business establishments, events, or locales is entirely coincidental. The publisher does not have any control over and does not assume any responsibility for author or third-party websites or their content.

ROGUE LAWMAN

A Berkley Book / published by arrangement with the author

PRINTING HISTORY
Berkley edition / September 2005

ISBN: 0-425-20523-1

BERKLEY®
Berkley Books are published by The Berkley Publishing Group,
a division of Penguin Group (USA) Inc.,
375 Hudson Street, New York, New York 10014.
BERKLEY is a registered trademark of Penguin Group (USA) Inc.
The "B" design is a trademark belonging to Penguin Group (USA) Inc.

PRINTED IN THE UNITED STATES OF AMERICA

10 9 8 7 6 5 4 3 2 1

1.

LAWDOG

THE dawn sky changed from black to pale blue-green as the three riders trotted across a sage-stippled bench in the very heart of the badlands, purple dust sifting behind them. The riders traversed a shallow stream and kicked their horses up the low cutbank spotted white with embedded bison bones.

Morning birds piped from gooseberry thickets and the sun burned through a low palisade of smoke-colored clouds along the horizon.

The lead horse jerked its head up and pricked its ears, agitated, white-ringed eyes giving a warning. Its rider, Deputy Marshal Gideon Henry Hawk, pulled back on the reins and looked around.

Directly behind him, Deputy Brit Hanley's dapple-gray chewed its bit and whinnied. "What the . . . ?"

"Smell something," Hawk said. At thirty-three, he was the senior deputy of the group. Broad-shouldered, slim-hipped, muscular as a stevedore, he had the light eyes and the high, wide cheekbones tapering to the anvil jaw of his mother's Nordic ancestors, and the dark hair and swarthy skin of his father, a Ute war chief. His saddle creaked as he sat up straight and brushed a seed from his bristly jaw with a ham-sized fist.

Deputy Luke Morgan sniffed the breeze, working his slender nose. "Wood smoke."

"That ain't all." The short Hanley, stocky and fat-faced but hard as a beer cask, raised the Winchester carbine he'd been carrying across his thighs, snugged the butt against his hip, and curled a gloved finger through the trigger guard. "My paint don't get a case of the fantods this bad less'n there's blood on the breeze."

"What say you, Gid?" Morgan asked. He was twenty-four, with a freckled, boyish face and cherry-red hair flowing down in girlish curlicues from his coal-black Plainsman that was nearly identical to Hawk's.

Hawk lowered his clear green gaze to the tracks they'd been following since leaving the little settlement of Phipp's Hill two hours earlier, at the first wash of dawn. Hawk made sure his stag-butted Colt Army and his nickel-plated Russian .44, both worn in the cross-draw position, showed brass, then slipped his Henry repeater from the saddle sheath under his right thigh, levering a fresh round into the magazine.

"The bastards picked up the stage trail ahead of us. I'll bet aces to eights they're at the roadhouse. Smoke's driftin' on the southeast breeze." He nodded south, his shoestring tie whipping around his bull neck in the breeze. "We'll ride Indian file, spread out. Keep your eyes peeled for lookouts."

Morgan shook his head and grinned. "Uh-uh. You're

wrong, Gid. I say they continued straight on. What we're smellin' is a deer carcass hung to season in some farmer's woodshed."

With a green silk handkerchief, Hanley wiped his nose, which always ran whenever he passed a chokecherry thicket. "The roadhouse is a long ride outta the way if we're only trackin' a dead deer, Gid."

Hawk gave them a quick glance of strained patience. "You younkers quit your gassin' and heel your mounts."

Hawk kicked his buckskin off the trail, heading southeast without looking back to see if the others followed.

"He thinks I'm just a dumb tinhorn," Morgan complained to Hanley. "I was right about that pretty little dove in Phipp's Hill, wasn't I? She *did* know French! Ha!"

Laughing, he and Hanley gigged their horses after Hawk.

The three lawmen trotted their horses through a spindly cottonwood copse and turned through a fold in the high, brown hills. Riding point, Hawk was rounding a bend in a dry wash when, hearing air sucked through gritted teeth, he turned his horse suddenly left and sawed back on the reins. A man crouched atop the butte above the wash, aiming a Spencer rifle.

"Brit! On your *left*!"

The young Hanley ducked as a rifle barked. The slug tore his gray felt hat from his black curls. Calmly, holding his reins in his left hand, Gideon Hawk raised the Henry in his right, aimed, and fired.

The slug took the man through the middle of his chambray shirt, puffing dust. He grunted and stiffened as his shabby bowler rolled off his shoulder. He dropped his rifle, fell to his knees, then rolled down the butte, piling up in the wash like a fresh cow pat.

"Jesus H. Christ!" Morgan exclaimed, glancing at Hanley's hat. Lying atop a sage clump, it sported a round hole through the crown—front and back. "You hadn't ducked, that woulda been your head!"

Hawk reined his horse in a taut circle as he gazed around for more lookouts.

"Thanks, Gid," Hanley said, glancing sheepishly at the older man. He dismounted to retrieve his hat. "How'd you spot him, anyway?"

"Heard him," Morgan said knowingly, grinning. "They say ole Gid's got the ears of a bat and the eyes of a prairie falcon."

Hawk turned his head to them sharply, holding two fingers to his thick black mustache. "Come on," he whispered, heeling the buckskin forward as he swung his gaze back and forth across the well-traveled stage road they'd picked up.

They rode through the gradually widening ravine until several buildings opened before them, in a brushy hollow. A two-story, log-and-adobe house sat against a steep bluff, with a sign over the wide front porch announcing FOOD/WHISKEY/GIRLS. To the left, across the two-track stage road, sat a barn, several outbuildings, and two corrals in which several horses milled. Above the barn's gray doors, the words EAGLE CANYON STAGE STOP AND ROADHOUSE were painted in large, green, sun-faded letters.

Dropping his gaze, Hawk saw that the yard before the cabin had been recently churned by fresh boot prints. Glass from shattered beer and whiskey bottles lay amidst the prints. Brass bullet casings winked in the bright morning light.

What captured the brunt of the lawman's attention was the dead man lying facedown in the middle of the stage road. He was short and stocky, with longish black hair. That was about all Hawk could tell about him, because the body was nearly covered in dried blood.

The right hand had been blown away, leaving a fly-blackened stump and exposed bone shards. All the fingers of the left hand had been shot off. The pieces lay nearby, like small, bloody sausages. What Hawk assumed to be the man's leather-brimmed watch cap lay across the trail, riddled with bullet holes.

"Good Christ," Deputy Morgan said.

"Spread out," Hawk ordered.

As the men separated, the squeak of a rusty hinge sounded. Hawk snapped his eyes to the cabin. A second-story shutter swung slowly open, and a rifle jutted from the open window, parting the curtains.

"Down!" Hawk yelled.

The rifle cracked as Hawk kicked his boots free of his stirrups and hit the ground on his right shoulder. Rolling as another crack sounded, he lighted on his butt, extended the Henry, and fired two quick rounds. One round shattered the window. The other barked and sparked off the rifle barrel. A man cursed. The rifle disappeared, and the curtains dropped back over the window.

"Take the porch!" Hawk yelled to the other two deputies. "I'll cover you!"

As Hanley and Morgan bolted out from behind the stock trough and a sage clump, running toward the cabin,

Hawk snapped off four shots at the window. The slugs plinked through the glass or thudded into the casing.

He lowered the rifle and cast his green-eyed gaze at the porch. Both deputies had made it. Rifles held at port, they pressed their backs to the front wall between the door and a large window on the left.

Firing another shot, Hawk bounded to his feet and sprinted onto the porch. He glanced at the two younger men. The taller, wiry Morgan had lost his hat, and a wing of thick red hair nearly covered his right eye. Wide-eyed and flushed, both men watched Hawk, awaiting his lead.

Hawk threw open the screen. The inside door was open. Bounding inside, he sidled left and raised his cocked Henry to his shoulder, sweeping the barrel from right to left as his eyes adjusted and as the other two deputies thundered in behind him, breathing hard.

He quickly raked his eyes across the room. The dozen or so tables were haphazardly shoved together or scattered. Several tilted to the floor over broken legs. Playing cards, glasses, and bottles littered the tobacco-stained sawdust sprinkled over the rough-pine puncheons.

Hanging from one nail on the far left wall was a portrait of Adam and Eve, obscured by bullet holes around the frolicking couple's privates. Along the far right wall, a makeshift plank bar fronted rough-pine cabinets and stacked fruit crates. Spying a human form in the periphery of his vision, Hawk wheeled toward the bar, rifle extended and slanting toward the floor. A man cowered behind the right-most barrel holding up the pine planks, not far from the door.

"You! Up!"

The man grunted and sighed as he climbed to his

feet—a fat man in a long deerskin apron and with round-rimmed spectacles. His shaggy beard was tobacco-streaked. His eyes found the badges on the newcomers' vests, and he heaved a sigh.

"Glad to see you boys! Did you see what they did to my hostler out there?"

"Where are they?" Morgan asked, eyeing the low, wainscoted ceiling.

The man jerked his head at a Z-frame door at the back of the room. "Two in there. Two upstairs. My workin' girls are with 'em."

"There a back door?" Hawk asked.

Dabbing at his sweat-shiny forehead with a filthy handkerchief, the fat man nodded. "Behind the stairs."

Hawk said, "Brit, go around and watch the back door. Luke, watch the stairs."

Hanley turned and jogged out the front door. Breathing hard, squeezing his rifle in both hands, Morgan said, "What're you gonna do, Gideon?"

Moving slowly toward the door at the back of the room, rifle extended before him, Hawk said, "I'm gonna say hidy to our friends back here."

"They shouldn't be much trouble, after all they drank last night," said the fat barman, cowering again behind the beer keg, which wasn't wide enough to shield him completely. He added, "Please don't hurt the Mex girls. They really bring the cowpokes in of a Saturday night."

As Hawk stepped to the right side of the red door and pressed his back to the wall, Morgan moved to the bottom of the stairs and aimed his rifle up the steps. Hawk pounded the door with his rifle butt.

"U.S. marshals!" Hawk shouted.

His voice was still echoing when a loud explosion rocked the station, and a large, round hole appeared in the red door. Close on the first blast's heels came another, blowing away the latch and throwing the door wide open on its leather hinges.

"Oh, mercy!" trilled the barman.

Rifle raised, Hawk bolted through the open door. The room was dully lit by the sun through a single, red-curtained window. In a wink, he saw the three figures in the room—a man and a woman in the bed to his right, another man standing ten feet before him, naked save for a double-rig pistol belt.

Taller than Hawk's six-two, with raw Indian features and long black hair, the standing man tossed away his smoking, double-barreled shotgun and reached for the pistols on his naked hips.

"Grab iron and die!" Hawk warned.

The man raised the right pistol while shucking the left. Hawk's Henry barked twice, blowing the man back against a dresser, shattering the dusty mirror. The man groaned and fired two shots into the floor as he fell.

Conscious of shouts and booming gunfire upstairs, Hawk swung to the man on the bed. He was as big as the Indian, with a broad, pitted face charred dark red by the sun, and a tight cap of curly orange hair. Around his chest swung a gold medallion. He sat straight up in bed, holding the chubby Mexican girl in his lap and pressing the broad blade of a razor-sharp bowie knife to her throat. Her pale, naked breasts rose and fell as she panted, horrified.

"Drop it or I'll cut her head off!"

A seasoned lawman, Hawk knew that if he dropped the

Henry, neither he nor the girl would be around for late-morning coffee. He drew a bead on the man's left temple. The man saw it coming. His eyes widened and his jaw dropped as Hawk's Henry belched smoke and flames.

The red-haired man's head snapped back, violently smacking the wall behind him, streaking the pink, flowered wallpaper with brains and blood. He slumped onto a shoulder, snapping his jaws open and closed as he died. Sobbing breathlessly, the girl scrambled off the bed and folded up against the wall, her head in her hands.

Hawk lowered his rifle and glanced at the ceiling. From upstairs came the thunder of running feet and furious shouts. Two shots were popped off, followed by loud cursing.

Wheeling on one heel, Hawk bolted from the room and up the stairs, taking the steps three at a time while ejecting a spent shell and feeding a fresh round into his rifle's chamber. At the top of the stairs, he stopped and stared down his rifle barrel at the narrow, dim hall, which smelled of sex, booze, and gun smoke.

At the end of the hall, near an outside door, lay a man clad only in buckskins, a silver-plated pistol lying near his bare feet. Blood gushed from two holes in his chest. His open eyes were death-glazed, reflecting the light from the window behind him. Through the open door to the man's left, a girl's round face appeared, wide-eyed with terror. Seeing Hawk, she gasped and withdrew back into the room.

Hawk shuttled his gaze right. Shadows moved against an open door halfway down the hall.

"Drop the damn gun or I'll kill him!" a man shouted inside the room.

"You ain't gettin' outta here!" Luke Morgan yelled.

"Drop it!"

A brief pause, then Morgan said, "Calm down—I'm dropping it!"

Hawk ran down the hall and turned into the room, sweeping his raised rifle around. Before him, his back to him, was Luke Morgan, bent forward, his pistol in his right hand, six inches from the floor.

Facing Hawk and Morgan was a wiry Mex clad in blue denims and a grimy undershirt. His face and arms were grotesquely, brightly tattooed. He was shielding himself with Deputy Brit Hanley, who was bleeding from a wound in his right shoulder. In the Mex's right hand was a pearl-gripped Colt Lightning, hammer cocked, barrel jammed against Hanley's right temple.

Hearing Hawk behind him, Morgan froze in his crouch and glanced back over his right shoulder. The Mex's eyes flicked to Hawk and he tightened his grip on Hanley's collar.

"I'm gonna kill this sumbitch, you don't drop those irons!"

"Don't do it," Hanley sobbed, tears dribbling down his cheeks. "He'll kill us all. . . ."

"Brit's right," Hawk told Morgan as he tried to draw a bead on the Mex's head. The Mex ducked behind Hanley, who was broader than the man behind him. Hawk couldn't get enough separation between the two to risk a shot.

"Soon as you drop those irons, I'm out the window," the Mex yelled, jerking his head to indicate the open window behind him. Jamming his Colt even tighter against Brit's temple, he shouted, "Throw 'em down!"

Hawk glanced at Morgan, who'd straightened, his pistol in his hand. Hawk glanced at Morgan and shook his head. "Luke, we give up our guns, we give up our ghosts."

"I'm countin' to three," the Mex shouted, backing toward the window, pulling Hanley with him. Veins bulged in his thin neck and forehead. "I don't see your guns on the bed, I'm drillin' a slug through this lawdog's *head*!"

Morgan glanced at Hawk behind him, then sighed and tossed his .45 on the mussed bed to his right.

"You, too, *hombre grande*!" the Mex yelled at Hawk.

"Goddamnit, Luke."

"Don't do it, Gid," Hanley begged.

"One!" the Mex shouted. *"Two!"*

"Goddamnit!" Hawk grated out as he lowered his rifle and chucked it onto the bed.

The Mex smiled, drawing his thick lips savagely back from his small brown teeth. A savage light glittered in his brown eyes like rubies at the bottom of a murky stream.

"No!" Morgan shouted.

At the same time, the Mex squeezed the Lightning's trigger. Hanley's head snapped hard to the left, blood spurting from the hole in his right temple.

Whooping insanely, the Mex dropped Hanley and extended his pistol at Morgan and Hawk. Both lawmen dove for cover as the Mex fired two quick rounds, then turned and leapt through the window. Behind the bed, Hawk rolled off his right shoulder and turned to Morgan, who'd leapt left, overturning a washstand and a chair.

"Luke?" Hawk inquired.

"Son of a bitch!" Morgan cried, climbing to his feet, apparently unharmed. His wide eyes were glued to Han-

ley, slumped on the floor before the window, a blood pool
growing around his head.

Hawk had climbed to a knee before he felt a hot ache
in his right arm, and his stomach turned with nausea. His
eyes fluttered, and he dropped forward on his hands.
Blood splattered onto the floorboards beneath him.

Beyond the window rose the thud of someone hitting
the ground, followed by the Mex's cry, *"Mierda!"*

Blinking his eyes to clear his head, Hawk saw Morgan
scoop his pistol off the bed and kneel beside Hanley.

"Brit," Morgan whispered, gritting his teeth.

Cursing, he rose and bolted toward the window. He
poked his head and pistol outside, froze, then climbed on
through.

Cursing and holding his wounded right arm, Hawk
gained his feet, glanced at Hanley slumped on the floor,
and walked to the window. He swept the curtain aside and
cast his gaze at the yard beyond the overhanging porch
roof.

The Mex was down on his right hip, clutching at his
right leg, that foot turned at a sharp angle from the ankle.
The Mex's pistol lay ten feet away.

Morgan was still crouched where he'd landed in the
yard, his gun aimed at the Mex. Slowly, he straightened
and walked stiffly toward the injured killer, his .45 held
before him, hammer drawn back.

"Hold on, Luke. I'll be right down," Hawk grated out
as, wincing against the pain in his arm, he grabbed his
rifle off the bed and strode into the hall.

He descended the stairs two steps at a time, passed the
barman sweating behind his makeshift bar, and stepped
outside.

"Hold on, Luke," Hawk repeated.

Morgan was on one knee beside the Mex, holding his .45 to the man's right temple. The Mex winced and cut his fear-sharp eyes between Hawk and the cocked revolver.

"I'm gonna kill this greaser, Gid." Morgan's words sliced out through gritted teeth. "He's gonna get as good as he gave Brit!"

The Mex just stared up at him, challenge mixing with the fear in his dung-brown eyes.

Hawk walked up behind Morgan. Standing over him, he said, "No Judge Lynch, Deputy. Remember what we talked about? You ain't the executioner."

"We can't let this vermin live . . . not after what he done to Brit!"

"He'll go before a judge and jury, and *then* he'll hang."

Morgan shook his head slowly and stared down at the Mex. "Brit's wife's in the family way. She'll be due next month. He'd have been a father, and a damn good one. And this punkwood took his life away." He paused, the walnut-gripped .45 trembling in his hand. "What's his wife gonna do now? What's his child gonna do? 'Cause o' *this*?"

"Brit gave himself over to the law. He knew the risks. You do, too. The frontier's full of bottom-feeders like this one here. Let him stand trial. He'll hang."

Morgan's gun hand shook. Hawk saw the kid's cheeks dimpling where his jaws hinged.

"What's the point? We saw him do it. Witnesses in town saw him and the others kill those bank tellers." Morgan turned to look over his shoulder at Hawk.

"Who's to know if we just killed him and threw him in a ravine, let the hawks and wolves take care of him?" He sobbed. Tears dribbled through the dust and sweat on his clean-shaven cheeks. *"Who'd know?"*

Hawk reached down and put his hand on the kid's shoulder. Firmly he said, "It's the law, Deputy. Now, ease that hammer down and holster your weapon."

Morgan looked at the Mex. The Mex's eyes slitted as he grinned. Morgan jammed the gun barrel harder against his head and cursed. Bald fear flashed in the Mex's eyes.

Finally, Morgan pulled the gun away. He depressed the hammer, tipped the barrel skyward, and released his grip on the Mex's shirt. Pushing off his bent knees, he slowly stood.

The Mex grinned mockingly up at him, his lips trembling from the pain of his broken ankle. "I'm gonna need a doctor. That's how the law works, huh? Fix my ankle before you hang me?" The taut grin widened.

Turning to Hawk, Morgan scowled. "This one ain't worth it, Gid. You can tell Lucinda Hanley what he done to Brit."

Hawk looked at the Mexican, then plucked his handcuffs from the back of his cartridge belt and held them out to Morgan. "Cuff him."

Morgan grabbed the cuffs, knelt down, and gave the sneering Mex a strong left jab. The smile was gone as the Mex spat blood in the dirt. "I was just turnin' him around," the deputy said to Hawk.

2.

NED

TWO weeks later . . .
   Tipping their hats low against the wind, five riders trotted their horses along a stage road through a shallow prairie swale. The wind blew their dusters straight out behind them and caused their horses to fidget and hesitate, subtly imploring their masters for a quiet barn out of the stinging sand and tumbleweeds.

Rounding a bend, the lead rider reined his paint to a halt. The others followed suit, stared out from under their low hat brims at the tall, gray building sitting forty yards ahead, on a grassy hill shrouded in windblown dirt and sand.

"This the place, Ned?" one of the others asked the leader, raising his voice above the wind's howl.

The leader didn't say anything. He was a swarthy, slender man dressed like a gambler in a flashy suit, with a brocade vest and bowler. He had a face like alligator skin, with eyes set too close together and a wide, crooked nose. The hair blowing out from his shoulders was bone-white, in sharp contrast to his Indian-dark complexion. That and his weathered countenance conspired to make him look much older than his actual forty.

"What time is it, Crazy Chuck?" he asked without turning his head to the others.

"Why in the hell you keep askin' me the time, Ned?" Crazy Chuck asked, holding his battered Stetson on his head with both hands.

"Shut up and give me the time." Ned stared at the unpainted building looming atop the rise. A shutter banged and the sign hanging below the porch moaned like a slow-dying cat.

Crazy Chuck plucked a battered turnip from his vest pocket, flipped the lid, and crouched over the face as he cupped the watch from the blowing sand. "It's ten minutes past the last time you asked." He snapped the watch closed and stuffed it back in his pocket.

Scowling against the weather, Ned Meade heeled his horse into a walk. The others did likewise.

Crazy Chuck turned to Johnny "Beaver Face" Pyle riding on his right. "What the hell's with Ned and my friggin' watch? I always knowed him to live for the moment."

The bucktoothed Pyle removed his frayed slouch hat and slapped it across Crazy Chuck's shoulder. "His brother's due to hang at high noon, ye wooden-headed dung beetle!"

Crazy Chuck watched Pyle trot ahead of him, climbing the steep rise to the house behind Ned Meade, Ken Dawson, and Lucius Running Bear. "Oh . . . shit," Crazy Chuck said, giving his own mount the spurs.

Meade and the others reined their horses up to the hitch rack before the tall, unpainted house and the swinging sign announcing simply MR. THOMAS'S PLACE in crude streaks of runny, yellow paint. The wind gnawed at the unpainted planks, threatening to pop the nails out and nudging the entire shack back and forth on its rickety frame. As Meade dismounted, casually holding his hat down with one gloved hand, two wooden shakes tore loose from the porch roof and blew away in the wind, heading east like tiny paper kites.

Leaving their horses to the mercy of the weather, Meade and the others crossed the porch and walked inside. Meade removed his hat and looked around the low, dim room, which held a few round tables to the right, around a smoky woodstove, and several display cases and shelves of cluttered dry goods to the left. At the back was a high bar fronted by pickle barrels and topped with two five-gallon jars of pickled eggs and ham hocks.

The place smelled like raw meat and vinegar and rancid buffalo hides.

"Mr. Thomas!" Meade called.

He called several times, looking around, before a back door opened and a man no taller than a candy barrel or a five-year-old child walked in, his pudgy arms filled with brown beer bottles. His legs were fat little pistons clad in denim overalls, the cuffs of which were shoved down in his tiny, black cowboy boots.

He had a scraggly goat beard on his chin, and wore a red plaid shirt, a black silk neckerchief, and a broad-brimmed black hat. His body was that of a dwarf, but his head was nearly normal-sized, sporting red-blond muttonchop whiskers. His smug, haughty eyes were sunk

deep under bushy brows. His nose was broad as a
doorstop.

"Hey, there, Shorty!" Crazy Chuck hooted, chuckling
at the little man who, casually raking his eyes across the
group, waddled behind the bar and stooped down to gentle the beer bottles onto the floor. "You run this place all
by your little lonesome?" Crazy Chuck asked, his voice
filled with laughter.

Meade and the others said nothing. Gathered before
the door, they cast their gazes under the bar. The little
man had set the beer on the floor and was now depositing
each bottle into an icebox standing as high as the top of
his hatted head.

"What's the matter, Shorty?" Crazy Chuck asked, befuddlement mixing with the humor in his eyes. "Cat got
your tongue?"

Crazy Chuck looked at Meade and the others. Seeing
the disapproval in his compatriots' eyes, he frowned.
"What?"

Beaver Face Pyle shook his head and sighed, his two
front teeth biting down on his well-chewed lower lip.

Behind the bar, the little man closed the icebox door,
brushed his hands on his pants, and ambled out toward
the center floor, limping deep as an old trapper with
"river joints."

"Ned, where the hell you been keeping yourself?" he
said, smiling as he approached Meade and holding out a
big, gnarled hand, half-moons of crud caked beneath the
nails. His voice squeaked like a rusty hinge.

"Mr. Thomas," Ned said, "good to see you again." He
canted his head to indicate the three men standing on his

left. "These boys are Beaver Face Pyle and Ken Dawson. The half-breed's Lucius Running Bear."

"New blood, eh, Ned?" Mr. Thomas said, shaking the half-breed's hand.

"You might say that."

"Who's this one?" He'd limped over to stare up at Crazy Chuck.

"Chuck Holbrook from out Wyoming way, otherwise known as 'Crazy Chuck.'"

"Crazy Chuck," the little man said with a nod. "You're s'posed to be faster'n Clinton Harvey."

"True enough, Shorty. In fact, I'm—*owwww! Jee-sus!*"

The little man had turned quarter-wise to Crazy Chuck, lifted his little right foot, then smashed the tiny heel down hard atop the big man's toes. As the fire shot up Crazy Chuck's legs, he leapt back, hopping on his good foot and grabbing the butt of his pistol.

He had jerked the gun half out of its low-slung holster when a bee stung his balls. At least, it felt like a bee sting—cactus-point sharp and instantly numbing. He stumbled against the back wall, froze, and looked down.

The little man was holding a razor-edged, wide-bladed knife to his crotch. The slender tip of the up-curved blade had torn through Crazy Chuck's denims and his underwear. If it wasn't drawing blood, it was on the verge of doing so.

Sensing that the farther he tugged his Colt from its holster the more severely the knife would violate his scrotum, Crazy Chuck opened his hand and let the revolver settle back down in its sheath.

"Goddamn!" Crazy Chuck cried, panting and pressing

his head and back against the wall, trying to escape the probing pain in his crotch.

There was no surcease. The little man held the blade point firm, glaring up at Crazy Chuck with a devil's pinched eyes, red ears, and wrinkled nose. A humorless smile tugged at his mouth and goat beard as his nasally voice squawked, "The name's *Mister* Thomas. *Comprende?*"

Crazy Chuck grunted and stretched his lips back from his teeth, glancing at Meade and the others for help.

"I done told you, fool," Meade said, looking on with humor in his dull eyes. "You call my friend here Mr. Thomas. Not Shorty or Half-Pint or Stretch or anything else. It's Mr. Thomas."

"More than one man has learned the hard way," Mr. Thomas said, glaring up at Crazy Chuck, ears red as irons. "I've fed more men their own oysters than a Chiricowy squaw."

Soft sounds of complaint rose up from Crazy Chuck's throat as, head thrown back against the wall, he stared down over his cheekbones at the dwarf. "Sorry, Mr. Thomas. It won't happen again."

A smile blossomed on Mr. Thomas's face. "Glad to hear that." He took the knife away from Ned's scrotum and returned it to the sheath hanging down his back, under his shirt, from which he'd produced it so quickly. He ambled back behind the bar, leapt onto a crate, and leaning over his fists, peered over the bar with an amiable smile.

"Now, then, what can I get for you gents?"

Meade plucked a sucker from a wooden box and slouched into a spool-back, cane-bottom chair. "Information about a certain deputy United States marshal livin' in these parts," he said, removing the brown paper from around the sucker's purple head. "Gideon Henry Hawk."

"Hawk." The dwarf's head bobbed, as if the name had been a strain to get out. "I hate that son of a *bitch*!"

Meade licked the sucker, crossed his knees, and smiled. "He does live around here, then."

"He lives up in Crossroads, six miles up the road," the dwarf said, thumbing eastward and raising his voice above the wind's moan and the wall creaks. "Son of a bitch keeps a tight rein on my Injun trade. Somehow, he always seems to know when I'm about to make a trip over to the reservation with my whiskey. Those poor Injun bastards love my skull pop better'n life itself. You'd think that when people have so little and love somethin' so much, Hawk'd see fit to look the other way now and then. But does he?" Mr. Thomas shook his head, slinging his goat beard. "Pshaw! Big, mean bastard!"

The dwarf looked at Meade. "Cross you, did he, Ned?"

Meade said nothing for a time. The others fidgeted, glanced at the floor or the denims displayed on a wire rack.

"What time is it, Crazy Chuck?"

Holbrook fished his tarnished timepiece out of his vest pocket, and flipped the lid. He shaped his lips for a whistle, but no sound came out. Flushing, he turned to Meade. "It's just now noon."

The others turned to Meade. They didn't say anything. The wind created cross-drafts, which swayed a lamp over a table against the right wall beneath the stairs. Dust sifted from the ceiling beams.

"What's at noon?" Mr. Thomas asked.

Expressionless, staring straight ahead, Meade raised his left, three-fingered hand for silence. He kept it there. In the other hand he held the wet grape sucker. The dwarf frowned at him but kept his tongue.

The others bowed their heads.

Finally, Meade slowly lowered his left hand. "My little brother, Ted, was just hanged in the territorial capital."

The dwarf clucked and shook his head. "That's too bad, Ned. Jesus. That's tough. Little Ned-Ted. I remember him well."

"Hawk brought him in," grunted Lucius Running Bear, who was testing the fabric of a woman's dress between the thumb and index finger of his right hand. He lifted the material to his nose and sniffed.

Meade bit off a chunk of the sucker and chewed loudly. "Hawk walked into Ted's house one night, when Ted and his wife were in bed, sound asleep. Ted was unarmed and unaware. Hawk just stepped into his room, snugged his big pistol up to Little Ned-Ted's head, and thumbed the hammer back. Ted's wife was scared to death. Ted himself almost had a heart seizure. You remember how frail he is . . . was."

Staring at the scarred cottonwood planks before him, the dwarf nodded.

"Now, we all know about Ned-Ted's, uh, taste, for little boys." Meade held up his left hand and the chewed sucker in his right. "I ain't denyin' that. He had a problem, Ted did. But he was workin' on it. And I just don't believe he'd have killed that kid, like they said he done. Ned-Ted had his problems—we all of us do—but you can't tell me he chopped the boy up and threw him down that well."

"No, I can't believe that," Ken Dawson said, standing near a cracker barrel, his hands crossed before the big silver buckle of his cartridge belt. He shook his head without raising his eyes.

Meade raised the sucker. "Someone in Mandan was out to git him. Probably even planted chicken or pig blood on his coveralls, to make their story ring true."

"And them witnesses, they was paid off," said Crazy Chuck Holbrook, absently running a gloved hand over his crotch.

"And Hawk believed every word," Meade growled. He stared at the sucker, brought it slowly to his mouth, and bit off another small hunk.

"Hawk, huh?" The dwarf nodded, a cunning light flashing in his small blue eyes. "You gonna even the score, Ned?"

Crunching the sucker in his teeth, Meade nodded. "Tell me about Hawk. Where does he live? I hear he's married. How many kids?"

"Lives in a little pale-blue house on the south edge of town. It's just a little place with a porch and a stable and a garden out back. He got himself wounded a couple weeks back and is dealin' faro at the Dakota House most days till he heals. His wife's a golden-haired little waif. Kinda delicate, I hear. His boy, Jubal, is a pudgy little tyke." The dwarf tapped his temple. "Not cuttin' with a sharp knife. Has trouble in school. Other kids tease him."

Meade's eyes gained a thoughtful cast. "Jubal, eh?"

The dwarf nodded. "I was told his name was Jubal. Wife's name is . . . ?" He frowned and raked his stubby fingers through his beard. "What was her name now, anyway?"

Meade glanced at the sucker and took another bite. "That's all right, Mr. Thomas. I think you've given me everything I need to know about Marshal Hawk." He chewed, nodded, and swallowed. He glanced at his men. "Boys, I think it's time we paid us a little visit to Crossroads."

Meade had just gained his feet when a thunderous crash rocked the building. He clawed his silver-plated Remington from his holster and, legs spread, crouching, leveled the revolver at the building's rear.

The outside door had opened. The wind had slammed it against the outside wall. A tall figure—so tall he had to stoop under the frame—appeared with a load of wood balanced on one arm. The man reached back with the other hand and drew the door closed behind him as he entered the room, the top of the door frame raking the floppy cloth hat from his head.

Her head.

As the figure clomped into the room, shoulder-length, lusterless blond hair fell onto her shoulders. The woman was pale-skinned, gray-eyed, with a long face, heavy brow, and a chin sharp enough to hoe potatoes. She wore a flour-sack shirt under a man's threadbare suit coat missing all its buttons, and torn black trousers.

"Not to worry, gents," Mr. Thomas said, holding out his hands. "That's just my wife, Stretch." The dwarf cackled as the woman knelt to retrieve a log she'd dropped. "Ain't that a tall drink o' water?"

Meade and the others holstered their weapons, regarding the tall, drab woman with awe. She had to be over six feet tall.

"She's your wife, Mr. Thomas?" Meade asked, snapping the keeper strap over his Remington's hammer.

"Bought her off a farmer passin' through on his way to the goldfields up in Canada. She can't get pregnant, and he wanted kids, so he sold her to me for a sack of potatoes and an old Spencer rifle."

Crazy Chuck regarded the woman with interest. "Quite a deal, Shor—I mean, Mr. Thomas."

"She ain't nothin' special, but she makes it a little less quiet for me out here."

Mr. Thomas laughed, leapt off his crate, and ran out from behind the bar. The woman had retrieved the fallen log and had turned toward the woodstove in the right center of the room. Head down, the dwarf bulled into the tall woman's backside, mashing his face against her rear.

The woman howled and stumbled forward, dropping the logs, tripping over them, and falling to her hands and knees. She whipped a look over her shoulder, brows beetled, lips pursed. "G-goddamn you, Mr. Thomas! Wha-what'd you g-go and do that for?"

Mr. Thomas laughed and turned to his visitors. "When she came here, she thought she could run things, kick me around. Ha! I lay the law down every day, boys, and she calls me *m-m-m-mister!*" He slapped his thigh, laughing.

"That's a helluva relationship you two have," Meade told him.

The others laughed. The woman was cursing under her breath and gathering the wood.

"You boys can take her upstairs for a poke," Mr. Thomas said. "It'll cost you two dollars apiece, but look at her, that's a lotta girl for two dollars!"

"Thanks, anyway, Mr. Thomas," Meade said, tossing

his sucker stick into a sandbox brown with tobacco quids. "But we have to get movin'."

"Stretch'll spread her legs for one dollar apiece," Mr. Thomas called as the men headed for the door.

"Hey," Crazy Chuck said, indignant. "How come you can call her Stretch but no one can call you—"

Meade cleared his throat loudly and shoved Crazy Chuck through the door.

"'Cause I'm meaner'n a diamondback in a privy pit!" Mr. Thomas called after them.

Meade's men were mounted on their windblown mounts, holding their hats on their heads and reining the horses away from the hitch rack, when Crazy Chuck shook his head and said, "You boys go on. I just can't let that go. That little ringtail stuck a blade to my *balls*!"

"What're you doin', Crazy Chuck?" Meade called above the wind and pelting sand.

"Go on!" Crazy Chuck yelled, slipping out of his saddle, loose-tying his reins to the hitch rack, and mounting the porch steps.

Squinting against the wind, Beaver Face turned to Meade. "What we gonna do, Boss?"

Meade just stared at the door, which opened five seconds after Crazy Chuck had stepped through it. Crazy Chuck stumbled out onto the porch backward. The door slapped closed.

Crazy Chuck turned toward the road, and Meade winced. Mr. Thomas's pig-sticker protruded from Crazy Chuck's throat. The gunman's Colt was in his right hand. As he stumbled down the steps, he fired it three times into the floor, the reports sounding like distant twig snaps beneath the roaring wind.

Crazy Chuck slumped down against a porch post, sat for several seconds, blood gushing from his throat and bibbing his chest, then fell slowly onto his right shoulder.

Mr. Thomas stepped onto the porch, his goat beard blowing in the wind. He looked down at the dead gun-man, shook his head, then waddled down the steps and, propping one foot against the dead man's left shoulder, yanked the knife from his throat.

He cleaned the blade on Crazy Chuck's shirt and turned to Meade, watching from his saddle. "Sorry, Ned," the dwarf said.

Meade held up his hands. "That's all right, Mr. Thomas. Crazy Chuck had it comin' for I-don't-know-how-long. His horse is yours, if you need an extry."

Mr. Thomas saluted with the knife.

"Three Fingers" Ned Meade and the others rode off into the wind and blowing sand.

3.

JUBAL

IN the kitchen of her family's one-and-a-half-story frame house on Cottonwood Street, Linda Hawk shoveled green beans onto her son's plate and said, "Good beans from your momma's garden. Eat up, Jubal."

The wind pelted the windows with sand and made the walls tick and groan.

"Aw, Mom," ten-year-old Jubal Hawk said. "I didn't ask for more beans, just more potatoes and gravy."

"If you're going to have more potatoes and gravy, you have to have just as many more green beans. A growing boy like you needs plenty of vegetables." Linda Hawk turned to her husband. "Isn't that right, Pa?"

"That's right, Jube," Gideon Hawk said as he poured himself more coffee from the large, speckle-blue pot. He used his left hand, as the wounded right one was still confined to the white sling around his neck. The wound had been healing, but the doctor had warned him not to remove the sling for another week. "Gravy just makes you fat." The big lawman reached over and lightly poked his son's fleshy side. The boy recoiled, laughing. His father wrapped a hand around the boy's pale, undefined left bicep. "Green beans give you *muscle*!"

"If I eat green beans, will I get arms big as yours, Pa?"

"Sure you will."

Jubal bunched his lips and frowned down at his beans. He poked one with his fork and reluctantly stuck it into his mouth. Chewing, he said, "Will my brain get bigger, then, too?"

Hawk was sipping his coffee. He glanced at Linda, standing at the small kitchen counter and cutting into the rhubarb pie she'd baked that morning. Linda caught the glance and held it. She had long, thick, naturally curly hair and soft blue eyes. Her fine, high-boned face was splattered with light freckles.

Gideon turned to the boy. "What's that, son?"

"Teddy Roach said I must have a brain like a peanut. That's why it takes me so long to catch on to the readin' and cipherin' we're learning at school."

The boy's blue eyes—the same shade as his mother's—regarded Gideon sadly. He was a chubby, suntanned, handsome child. The childlike goodness and innocence fairly radiated from him. The lawman glanced at his wife again. Her eyes were glazed with tears. One slipped down, and she brushed it away, leaving a few grains of piecrust, and said, fighting the trembling in her voice, "Jubal, Teddy Roach had no good reason to say that to you! He was just being mean."

"Don't pay any attention to him, son," Hawk said.

"I should say don't listen to him," Linda said, her face turning pink, the tiny freckles darkening. A Texan by birth, she drawled faintly. "Why, Mrs. Craft was just tellin' me the other day how much you've been improving lately. She said that essay you wrote about the fish was one of the best in the class."

"That was 'cause you stayed up half the night helpin' me write it," Jubal said, staring down at his plate. He buried his fork in the gravy-covered potatoes and brought a load up to his mouth.

"Those were your ideas," Linda said. "I just helped you . . . organize them."

"I think Mrs. Craft gets frustrated, havin' to help me extra with my math. Teddy's right. My brain is peanut-sized." Jubal looked at Hawk. "Pa, will the beans help it get bigger?"

Hawk laid a big hand on the boy's head and leaned over him. "Son, the beans'll help everything about you grow fine and strong. But you have to stop listening to Teddy Roach. He's just tryin' to make you feel bad. You're as smart as anyone else. It just takes some folks a little longer to get a handle on things."

The boy grinned up at his father, gravy and potatoes staining his chin. "I'll keep eatin' my beans."

"Keep eatin' your beans," Gideon said. He tussled the boy's short, brown hair. "How 'bout we go fishin' after school?"

"Heck, yeah. We'll catch even more perch than we did last time!"

"You bet we will."

Linda brought two pieces of the rhubarb pie to the table, and set one before Gideon and one before Jubal.

She squatted down beside the boy, wrapped an arm around his shoulders, and kissed his cheek hard with a mother's passion. She stood and glanced at Gideon as she collected his dinner plate.

When the boy had finished his pie and collected his books, he gave each of his parents a parting kiss and opened the kitchen's outside door, his overalls and spruce-green shirt buffeted by the wind. "I'll see you after school, Pa!"

"See you later, Jube. Don't blow away!"

When the boy had gone, Linda turned from the range, where she was scrubbing a pan in the wreck tub. "That boy breaks my heart, Gid. He turns me inside out sometimes, I swear!"

Hawk cleaned up the last of his pie and whipped cream, tossed back his coffee, and removed his napkin. He stood and moved to his wife, wrapped his good hand around her waist. "He's a tough boy. Texas maverick stock from your side. He'll grow up to be a strong, good man. Don't worry about him."

"Well, he *is* slow," Linda said, turning her head but keeping her hands in the warm, soapy water. "And it just *kills* me when the other boys tease him. I could wring their scrawny necks!"

"You want me to talk to Teddy Roach's father?"

"Do you think it would help?"

"Not really. The boy needs to fight his own battles. But if you're really worried, I'll go and have a talk with Roach."

She ran the back of her hand across her chin, glanced out the window left of the range, and shook her head. "No," she sighed. "You're right. He has to fight his own battles." She glanced up at her husband and narrowed her eyes. "But just let me catch that little Teddy Roach alone in back o' the schoolhouse . . . !"

"Now, dear," Gideon said with a snort. He kissed her. "Don't you worry. Jubal's just a little softheaded, like your pa—"

"Gideon Hawk!"

The lawman raised his left hand in supplication and grinned. "And look how well that old goat did for himself."

He kissed her again. She kept her thin, soft lips closed, but a grin pulled at the corners. Gideon grabbed his gun belt off a wall peg. "I best get back to the saloon. Since Jubal and I are going fishing, we probably won't be home until supper time."

He swiped his black hat off another peg, snugged it over his thick, auburn hair, and scooped his faro box off the floor. Between his assignments as a deputy U.S. marshal—which paid little better than what an ordinary cowhand earned—Hawk dealt faro at the Dakota Hotel on Main Street in Crossroads.

Holding the door open, Gideon stopped and turned to Linda, frowning down at the wreck pan as she worked, biting her lower lip. The boy worried her something fierce, and constant worry and doting weren't good for a girl with her delicate constitution. Too often she couldn't sleep at night, and often took to bed with fevers.

Hawk set the faro box down, walked to her, turned her around, and kissed her hungrily. She wrapped her arms around him, returning the kiss. He ran his hands down her back, feeling the gentle curves and delicate bones. A small, frail, high-strung girl, like her mother.

"I love you, Gideon Hawk," she said, staring up at him.

"I love you, too. And don't you worry about that boy. He's one to ride the river with."

He kissed her again and winked. "Now, don't you go fixin' supper and jinx our fishin'."

She laughed as he turned to the door, grabbed the faro box, and walked out into the keening wind, clicking the door shut behind him.

Meade, Pyle, Dawson, and Running Bear entered the little town of Crossroads about twenty minutes after Gideon Hawk had returned to his faro table in the Dakota Hotel. Heads bent against the wind, the riders reined their horses to a halt before the feed barn and studied the three-story hotel up the street on their left.

Two men in ranch garb had just left the feed barn, and were angling across the street, bandannas whipping around their necks, toward the hotel. Just before they mounted the boardwalk, a tumbleweed rolled into the taller of the two men.

"Dang wind!" he cried. "I'm goin' back to Tennessee!"

He placed his left boot on the boardwalk and gave his right leg a shake. The tumbleweed came loose, careening high in the air toward the blacksmith shop, as though making up for lost time. The tall drover followed the shorter one into the saloon, carefully drawing the glass door closed behind him. The wind was so loud that Meade couldn't hear the latch click.

Head hunkered low between his sloping shoulders, Lucius Running Bear said, "I say we go in, have us a drink or two, shoot the marshal, and blow on outta this backwater dump. Damn tired o' this wind."

"Now, let's not get impatient," Meade said, studying the saloon's dark windows, glinting silver with reflected sunlight as the wind shook their panes.

Ken Dawson turned to Meade. "What're you talkin' about, Boss?"

"I'm saying that acts of vengeance must be well planned and executed. They must be slow, precise, and merciless."

"Even when it's this windy?" Beaver Face Pyle said, his perpetually parted lips lined with grit.

Meade gigged his horse ahead and pulled up before the Crossroads Dry Goods, where an old woman in a cream dress embroidered with little yellow flowers was nailing a sign back onto the wall beside the door.

"Granny, can you tell me where the school is?" Meade yelled above the wind.

The old woman turned from the sign, which read FRESH MILK ALL DAY EVERY DAY. She frowned around the twopenny nails she held in her thin lips. "Mind your manners, ye son of a bitch! It's straight ahead and left, other end o' town." She turned back to the sign and gave a nail another wrap.

"Thank you, Granny," Meade called. The old woman didn't turn around as Meade and the others headed up the street, horses walking stiff-legged and wide-eyed against the wind.

The group rode to the end of Main Street. The school sat left of the road, on a hard-packed lot, the two tree swings near the outhouse squeaking to and fro. Shadows moved in the windows.

Meade reined his horse off the trail's right side and halted the big sorrel in a grove of whining cottonwoods. A creek gurgled back in the trees. Meade stared across the field at the white school beyond the road.

"What the hell we waitin' for?" asked Lucius Running Bear.

"Recess," Ken Dawson answered for Meade, grinning.

The men dismounted their horses and loosened the saddle cinches. Pyle and Dawson smoked. Running Bear chewed a braided tobacco plug the way most men ate jerky. Meade sat on a deadfall tree within the grove and stared across the road at the school. His face was expressionless. The brim of his black hat bent up and down in the breeze wending through the trunks.

"Maybe they ain't gonna get no recess," Beaver Face said after they'd been waiting twenty minutes. "On account o' the win—"

The school's front door opened. The teacher stepped out onto the high wooden steps. Holding her blouse closed at the neck, she glanced around, scowling. Several children stepped out of the school, wound around her, and descended the steps to the yard. Several more appeared. She called something after them, and the children ignored her as they poured out into the yard, calling and laughing, their hair blowing, their clothes buffeting, dust kicking up around their feet.

Meade waited five minutes; then he and the others tightened their saddle cinches, mounted their horses, and rode slowly out of the trees. They crossed the trail and reined up before the school, where three boys in coveralls and scuffed brogans played jacks in the tough, brown grass.

"Say, can anyone here tell me which boy is Jubal Hawk?"

"That's him over there," one of the boys said, barely glancing up at the riders as he played, intent on his game. "He always sits over there, whittling sticks and such."

Meade glanced at the portly little boy—thick-necked and short-haired and wearing a green shirt and suspenders—sitting under a sprawling cottonwood tree at the far west side of the yard. The tree churned and swayed over the boy, shunting shadows, gray-green leaves flashing silver in the wan light as they blew.

Meade and the others rode over and looked down at the boy, who was putting the final touches on a horse carved from ash. The boy held the horse up close to his face, deftly scraping the wood with the small, bone-handled pocketknife in his left hand. He stuck his tongue out as he worked.

"Boy, are you Jubal Hawk?" Meade asked.

The boy, not having heard or seen the men ride up to the tree, gave a startled jerk. He lifted his gaze up to the riders and settled it on Meade.

"Yes, sir," he said, canting his head and squinting.

Meade lowered his gaze to the horse. "What you got there, son?"

The boy glanced at the horse in his right hand. A smile blossomed on his face, and he held the carving up for Meade to inspect. "It's a buckin' bronc!"

"Well, sure enough it is," Meade said. The horse in the kid's hand was nearly perfect, right down to the detailing of the horse's hooves and cocked tail. "You like horses, do you, boy?"

"I sure do. My pa said he's gonna buy me a pony soon as he can afford one."

Meade scrubbed his three-fingered hand across the grain of his beard, his bone-white hair blowing around his bowler snugged low on his forehead. He glanced at the other men, a cunning light entering his eyes. Looking back down at the boy, he said, "As a matter of fact, that's what I'm here to talk to you about."

Staring up at the outlaw, the boy frowned and hung his jaw.

"Your pa sent us over here to fetch you. We told him about this pony we have for sale, and he thought it might make a right fine horse for his son. The price is right, and he wants you to have a look at it. He'd have come, too, but he's busy over at the hotel."

The boy's eyes had opened wide, but he didn't say anything.

"What do you say, son? You wanna come and have a look at our pony?" Meade glanced at Ken Dawson. "A pretty roan, he is. Give him time, and he'll look just like that bronc you been carvin'."

Dawson turned away and snickered.

The boy set the knife and horse down and climbed heavily to his feet. His short brown hair whipped in the wind. His ears and pale, fleshy face had turned pink with excitement. "Really, mister? My pa said I could have a pony?"

"Sure, sure. As long as you like him, that is. Your pa wouldn't want to buy you a horse you don't like."

"No, I reckon not."

"Crawl on up here, and we'll go have a look at this red pony."

"Where you got him?"

"Just down the road aways. Only a mile or so." Meade glanced at Running Bear. "Ain't that right, Lucius?"

"All right," Jubal said. "If my pa said I could." He turned to the school. "I reckon I better go tell Mrs. Craft I'll be gone for a bit."

"We already squared it with Mrs. Craft, son," Meade said. He dismounted and, grunting, hefted the thick youngster up behind his saddle.

A few seconds later, Meade, Jubal Hawk, and the other three men were cantering along the trail, heading west, the wind tearing away their dust as soon as their horses kicked it up.

4

THE NOOSE

"COME to buck the tiger, gentlemen?" Gideon Hawk asked the two men in miner's garb who approached his table with sudsy beer mugs in their dirty fists.

"I reckon," said the blocky-headed gent with close-cropped, salt-and-pepper hair, staring down uncertainly at Hawk's baize-covered faro board. "Arch here ain't never played before. . . ."

"No problem, Arch," Hawk said, shuffling the faro deck in his big hands. The doctor had told him he could remove the sling from his arm to play cards.

He'd removed his black frock and loosened his string tie. His crisp black Stetson sat on the chair beside him, beside his silver-plated Russian. He liked having the weapon handy, in case of trouble, and the silver showed up well in the saloon's shadows.

The saloon was nearly empty, only a few regulars standing at the bar watching the wind shepherd tumbleweeds down the street beyond the big front windows. In the back kitchen, the hotel's Italian cook sang as he butchered the ducks a couple hunters had brought in earlier and sold for a quarter apiece.

"Let me explain it to you," Hawk said as the miners pulled up chairs on the other side of the table. Hawk's hands moved expertly as he talked. "After shuffling and cutting the deck, I place the cards into the box, like so. I draw cards from this slit in the side of the box in pairs, faceup. As you can see, every card from ace to king is painted on the board. You simply place your money on the card of your choice. If the card you've bet on is drawn first, you lose. If it's drawn second, you win. If neither, you bet again."

Hawk let the information sink in, then added, "The top card is the 'soda' card, the last the 'hoc' card. There are twenty-five turns from soda to hoc, after which we start all over again."

"If we're still flush," Arch grumbled, furling his bushy, gray-blond brows as he studied the board.

"I deal a friendly game, gentlemen," Hawk assured them, again shuffling the deck. "I don't wield the pasteboards to get rich, merely for your entertainment and to keep my family fed between marshaling jobs . . . or until this wing heals."

"Mr. Hawk here's a U.S. marshal," the first miner told Arch. "I reckon he *must* deal a straight game."

Arch squinted at Hawk for several seconds before pulling a thin wad of greenbacks from his coat pocket. The wind rattled the window behind Hawk and caused the lamps to flicker. The lawman hadn't seen the group of flinty-eyed firebrands who'd passed the window twenty-five minutes ago, heading for the school.

"All right," Arch muttered. "I'll give it a try. Doesn't look like there's much else to do around here, since all the girls are still asleep upstairs."

Hawk was about to give the cards one more shuffle when hurried footsteps sounded on the boardwalk. He cast a glance over his right shoulder. A full-hipped woman in a gray shawl, with silver-streaked hair gathered in a French braid behind her head, pushed through the hotel saloon's glass door, blinking the windblown grit from her eyes.

Jubal's schoolteacher.

The stout woman's fleshy cheeks were flushed as her gaze swept the saloon. Landing on Hawk, her eyes snapped wide. "Marshal Hawk!" Standing before the door, she stared at Hawk, frowning and stammering, deeply troubled.

His right arm hooked around his chair back, Hawk squinted at her. Tensely, he dropped the faro deck on the board and pushed himself up from the table. "What is it, Mrs. Craft?"

"Jubal didn't come in from recess. When I asked the other boys, they said he'd ridden off with several men on horseback."

The bartender, J.T. O'Malley, who'd been stooped over a newspaper spread upon the mahogany bar, said, "Jubal rode away with men on horseback?" The big, blond man made a face as though he didn't believe it.

"Five or six men," the woman said, shaking her head and spreading her hands in bewilderment. "Jubal got on behind one of them and . . ."

Gideon grabbed his hat, slipped the Russian into the cross-draw holster on his left hip, and leaving the faro board and cards on the table before the incredulous miners, took the three steps to the door in one easy stride. "Which way did they head?"

The woman turned quickly, her eyes following Hawk as he strode past her to the door. "Straight east along the stage road. I thought maybe you knew—"

Hawk didn't wait for the rest. He pushed through the door and stepped onto the boardwalk, peering east through the windblown grit between the false fronts of Main. Chewing his lip, he looked around for a horse. Spying three saddle ponies tied to a hitch rack a block down the street, he tipped his hat low against the wind and began moving that way.

The hotel door clattered behind him. "I'll give you a hand, Gid," said J.T. O'Malley, raising his voice above the wind and jogging up beside Hawk, both men angling across the street toward the Sporting Life.

O'Malley had removed his apron and donned a denim jacket but no hat. He held his double-barreled Greener in his big right paw. His legs were as long as Hawk's, but he had to jog to keep up as the lawman mounted the boardwalk before the Sporting Life and slipped the reins of a white-socked dun from the hitch rack.

As he turned the horse toward the street, grabbed the saddle horn, and toed the left stirrup, O'Malley shouted through the batwings, "Hawk and O'Malley are borrowin' the dun and the paint out front. Urgent business!"

The barman grabbed the paint's reins and climbed heavily into the balking horse's saddle. Shifting the shotgun to his left hand and turning the paint with his right,

O'Malley peered eastward down Main. Hawk and the dun were lunging out of sight through the dust and tumbleweeds.

"Come on, horse . . . let's go!" the bulky barman yelled, leaning forward over the paint's neck.

Knowing it had a strange rider in its hurricane deck, the paint took several kicks to its ribs before, rearing half-heartedly and giving its head a final shake, it broke into a run after Hawk and the dun.

As Gideon rode low in the saddle, he whipped his gaze from side to side, looking for sign of Jubal and the strangers. The dun chewed up the trail, the frothy, tea-colored Wolf Creek flashing between the bending willows and cottonwoods on his right. On his left, prairie hogbacks rolled gently toward a jog of brown hills veiled by dust.

A mile from town, the stream eased away from the trail, chalky buttes closing on both sides. Rain spat from the low sky, and a sudden, powerful gust whipped Gideon's hat from his head. Losing sight of the hoof-prints he'd been following, Hawk reined the dun to a sudden halt, scouring the ground with his gaze.

The riders must have left the trail.

"Gideon!" O'Malley's voice rose as though from a long tunnel.

Hawk whipped his head back toward Crossroads. The bartender galloped toward him, shotgun in his right hand, the wind making a blond tumbleweed of his head. Extending the hand holding his reins, he indicated something over Hawk's right shoulder. *"There!"*

Gideon whipped back around, squinting against the pelting rain. On one of the knobby buttes a hundred yards away and on the left side of the trail stood a lone, dead cottonwood. The sprawling, barren branches swayed to and fro, like a stiff old lady dancing by bending her knees and spreading her arms.

Beneath a stout branch sat two horseback riders, silhouetted by the gray-purple sky behind them. The one on the left, wearing a checked coat and a bowler hat, his long bone-white hair blowing out from his shoulders, like corn silk in the wind, sat tall and straight in the saddle. The other was short and stout, sitting hunched upon a black horse with one white sock, his hands apparently tied behind his back.

Both men faced Hawk down the hill.

A cricket hopscotched along the lawman's spine, and electricity shot through his limbs. The stocky rider was Jubal. A noose had been dropped over Jubal's head, tightened around his neck. The rope was wrapped around the stout branch above the horses, tied off near the cottonwood's base.

The man with the long white hair waved his right hand broadly. Loosing a taunting whoop, the man swung his right hand back behind Jubal's horse.

"*No!*" Hawk cried, slamming his heels against the dun's ribs, urging the mount into a lunging gallop. Fifty yards down the trail, he reined the dun from the trace and up the steeply rising butte.

The tall man whipped his right hand forward, connecting soundly with the rump of Jubal's horse. Bolting off its rear legs, the horse bounded forward. The rope pulled taut, jerking Jubal straight back off the mount's rump and dropping him straight down, like a wheat sack dropped from a barn loft.

"No—goddamn youuuuu!" Hawk shouted, staring over the horse's head.

The boy fell several feet before the rope grabbed, jerking his stubby body perpendicular to the tree with such force that the branch bowed.

Jubal hung straight down from the branch, chin to his chest, shoes lashing at the bending weeds beneath the tree.

Staring down the butte at Hawk, the long-haired man raised a hand to the brim of his hat, then casually reined his paint around and disappeared down the other side of the butte.

The dun lost its footing in the slick grass, dropped to a knee, and whinnied. Hawk stabbed the dun's ribs with his heels, screaming, "Go, goddamn you, horse—*goooooooooo!*"

The horse shook its head as it regained its footing and bolted up the butte in lunging, uncertain bounds.

Thunder rumbled and lightning flashed. The rain fell in gray, wind-buffeted sheets.

"Oh, Lordy!" groaned O'Malley on the paint galloping up the butte behind Hawk.

As the dun slowed from exhaustion, Gideon leapt from the saddle and ran the last few yards to the crest. He clawed his Colt from his holster, fired a slug through the rope, then turned and opened his arms, catching the boy against him as he fell.

"Jubal," Hawk muttered as he dropped to both knees, lowering the boy gently to the rain-soaked weeds and whipping the noose from his neck. "Boy, do you hear me?"

He took his son's face in his hands, massaged the

fleshy cheeks as if to rub life back into them. Hawk's voice quaked. "Jubal . . ."

The boy's eyes were closed. His head lolled on his stretched neck, which was already blossoming purple bruises and bleeding where the rope had rubbed it raw. The boy's light brown hair lay flat against his head. Usually swarthy and tan, his face was bleached and drawn, tiny blue veins showing in his cheeks and in the darkening rings around his eyes.

A small folding knife fell from Jubal's pocket—a horn-handled barlow into which the boy had carved a bucking horse.

Hawk continued rubbing Jubal's rain-splattered cheeks and gently shaking his body, trying to rouse him, trying to get the lids to open.

"Jubal . . . please . . . goddamn it, Jubal . . . *say something!*"

The boy lay inert in his father's arms, a wan, knowing smile lifting the corners of the boy's partially open mouth, as if he were only asleep and pleasantly dreaming.

Hawk was not aware of O'Malley's hand on his shoulder, giving a sympathetic squeeze. Hawk cradled the soft, young body in his arms and rocked it from side to side as he cried. After a time, still holding the boy in his arms, Hawk gained his feet, stumbling, teetering. His expression hardened and his eyes turned black as he stood beside O'Malley and stared northward down the butte.

The bowler-hatted rider was descending a hill shoulder to an old horse trail, where three other riders waited in a loose clump amidst cottonwoods, all wearing yellow or tan rain slickers, shoulders hunched against the weather. Two of the three rode double.

The long-haired man rode into the group, splitting it down the middle, and gigged his horse into a trot, heading north. The others turned their mounts and followed him away from the cottonwoods, their horses kicking up clods of grass and mud as they disappeared over a cedar-stippled hogback.

Gideon Hawk's jaws were taut, his teeth showing white as pearls between his lips.

Lightning stabbed at the butte just east of Hawk and O'Malley, striking a jumble of boulders along the crest, throwing up blue sparks, smoke, and rock shards. Thunder cracked like enormous doors slamming.

"Take my boy back to town," Hawk told O'Malley, still staring after the riders. "I'm goin' after them."

"You can't, Gid," O'Malley said. "There's too many of 'em. If they don't git ye, this weather will."

Hawk had just turned northward, looking for the horses, when he heard a commotion on the trail side of the butte. He turned with Jubal's legs dangling over his right arm.

At the bottom of the hill, several riders had appeared—probably men from town who'd heard the story from Mrs. Craft and had come to help. Behind them, a black buggy with a wind-battered canopy appeared, splashing through the puddles along the trail that had nearly become a stream.

One of the horseback riders was extending an arm toward Hawk. Two riders turned their mounts off the trail and started up the butte, their horses slipping in the mud and slick grass.

It was the buggy that held Hawk's attention. Two women stepped down from it, on opposite sides. One was

Mrs. Craft, dressed in a wool cloak and opening a black umbrella. Hawk's own wife, Linda, stepped down from the side facing the butte. Wearing Hawk's old duster and a shapeless hat, she stared up at the butte for a brief moment before, seeing Hawk holding their dead son in his arms, she bolted across the trail and started running up the butte's steep grade, slipping, falling, and losing her hat. She regained her feet and continued, tearing at the weeds for purchase.

"Linda, no—stay there!" Hawk shouted down to her, the words ripped by the wind.

As the frail woman in the oversized duster kept coming, half-running, half-crawling up the rain-slick slope, Hawk turned another glance after the fleeing riders, his eyes sharp as bowie knives.

Three Fingers Ned Meade.

Whose brother had been hanged today in Yankton.

Hawk turned again and started down the hill toward Linda.

From beneath the cottonwood, O'Malley watched Hawk take careful, mincing steps sideways down the grade, slipping once and dropping to a knee but keeping Jubal in his arms, continuing on until he met his wife halfway down the slope, on the leeward side of a mossy boulder.

Linda's scream rose from beneath the thunder and pelting rain. Gideon knelt with the boy in his arms. Linda dropped and fell over the body, her shoulders quaking as she took Jubal in her own arms, screaming.

"What the hell happened?" asked one of the two horseback riders halting his dripping mount beside the barman.

O'Malley stared down the hill, eyes dull with emotion, his blond hair plastered to his head.

Thunder boomed like a cannon. Lightning lit the sky.

"All hell just broke loose," the barman said.

5.

QUEEN VICTORIA'S

L ATE that night, when the storm had passed, Three Fingers Ned Meade and his three jackals cantered their horses along an old horse trail and into the yard of a sprawling Victorian house.

All the house's downstairs windows were lit. The porch itself was lit with Chinese lanterns strung along the front rail. Delicate piano music tinkled behind the drawn red curtains of a far right window.

Across the puddled, leaf-strewn yard were several hay barns, corrals, and an adobe-brick bunkhouse nestled in shrubs. The bunkhouse windows were lit as well.

Meade and his companions halted their mounts at one of several hitch racks before the Victorian's broad veranda and dismounted. A half dozen other horses stood before the racks. When Meade's men had tied their own horses, they sloshed through the ankle-deep mud, mounted the steps under a sign that read in gaudy hand-lettering QUEEN VICTORIA'S, and pushed through the Victorian's front door.

Removing his hat and throwing his long, damp hair back from his shoulders, Meade led his companions through the foyer and into the parlor opening on his left. One hand on his Remington, Ned looked around the ornately decorated, dimly lighted room in which three men sat in gaudy chairs and sofas with scantily but richly dressed women.

There were more women than men, and the two extra girls were playing cards at a table near an oak staircase, their hair and faces done up, but wearing plain-looking night jackets. From another room behind Ned, the piano continued tinkling what sounded to Meade's educated ears like a Bavarian waltz.

"I thought I heard riders," said the bulky woman moving down the stairs at the far end of the room, trailing a hand along the bannister.

Meade only glanced at her. He'd locked stares with the man sitting on the fainting couch to his left. A plump, round-faced brunette straddled the man's right knee, leaning forward and nuzzling his neck. The man was thin and long-faced, with a sharp nose, and eyes nearly as close-set as Meade's. The man had a grisly scar beneath his chin, as though someone had tried carving out his voice box with a garden trowel.

"Meade," the man grunted, moving his right hand from the brunette's leg to his own thigh, about a foot from the hogleg on his hip. His thumb twitched.

"Drake."

The bulky woman crossed the room with the hip-

rolling, shoulder-swaying amble of an old bullwhacker.
"How the hell are ye, Ned? Haven't seen you in a while."

Meade tore his gaze away from Drake, offered the big
woman, dressed in man's blue denims, cream flannel
shirt, with a red neckerchief knotted around her neck, a
wooden smile and regal bob of his head. "How've you
been, Queen?"

"Still in business, ain't I?" Victoria said, glancing
down at Ned's feet. She looked around him to the others.
"Say, you boys wouldn't mind takin' your boots off on
the porch, would you? Me and the girls just cleaned the
carpets the other day. You know how hard it is to keep a
clean carpet in clay country?"

Meade looked down at his muddy boots. He glanced at
Drake, who was still staring at him hard.

"Come on, boys," Meade said with a distracted air.
"Let's shed our boots on the porch."

"I don't like walkin' around stocking-footed," said the
big Indian, Lucius Running Bear. "Makes me feel
naked . . . same way I feel without my gun."

"Shit, you Injuns run around barefoot all day long!"
jeered Ken Dawson as he, Running Bear, and Beaver
Face followed Ned out to the porch.

When the men returned to the parlor in their stocking
feet, Queen Victoria was waiting for them with a whiskey
bottle raised in her right hand and a bright smile on her
freckled face topped by a tight cap of curly blond hair.
"Boys, how 'bout a drink on the house, just for takin'
your boots off? Then I'll roust the other girls from their
beauty sleep, and you can dance the four-poster jig."

"I'll take that drink upstairs, Victoria," Ned said. "And

you don't have to roust any of the girls upstairs for me. This one with Drake'll do just fine."

He walked stiffly over to Drake and slipped his long-barreled .45 from his holster. Seeing the gun, Drake gave a start and slapped his own pistol's butt. He didn't get half the gun out of its holster before Meade's Remy spat fire.

The bullet drilled a hole through Drake's chest, just left of the man's heart, throwing him back against the sofa. With a shriek, the girl rolled off Drake's knee toward the sofa's other end.

"Goddamnit, Ned!" Queen Victoria shouted.

Drake looked up at Meade, the light slowly leaving his eyes. "Jesus Christ, Ned . . . we ain't s'posed to roughhouse in Queen Victoria's place."

"That wasn't roughhousing," Ned said, bending over the dying man, staring into his face. Behind him, his jackals stood with their hands on their pistol butts, facing Drake's men with warning looks on their faces. "I just killed you for double-crossing me in El Paso, you worthless pile of dog shit!"

"Goddamnit, Ned!" Victoria yelled again, fists on her hips. "I don't allow shootin' on the premises. Look at all that *blood*!"

Meade grabbed the bleach-faced brunette still staring dumbstruck at Curly Bill Drake. As he pulled the girl toward the stairs, he nodded to indicate Curly Bill's men and said to his own, "Take their guns and kick 'em the fuck outta here."

To the boys themselves, sitting stunned with their girls, Meade said, "I don't have no beef with you fellas.

A follower is only as good as the man he follows. But I'll kill you both if I ever see you after tonight."

Meade turned and took the stairs two steps at a time, the girl grunting and sobbing behind him, dropping to her knees. Meade pulled her up and half-dragged her to the second-story hall lit by red bracket lamps. When he asked her which room was hers, she looked at a door, and Meade pushed her through it, jerking the girl in behind him and throwing her onto the bed.

Forty-five minutes later, Meade was still pounding away between the girl's spread legs, grunting and sweating, his breath getting shallow. He was weary and growing wearier by the second. Satisfaction was just beyond his reach.

The girl stared up at him blankly. Sweat shone on her neck and in the valley between her pale breasts flattened against her chest.

"Maybe we should have a drink," she said.

"Shut up," Meade said, wincing and biting his lip, unable to understand what the problem was. He'd never had this trouble before. He'd always been able to take his satisfaction from a woman without any problem at all, even after a night of hard drinking.

He lifted his head and stared at the wall. An image shone before him, like a picture hanging above the bed: Gideon Hawk standing atop the hill, under the windblown cottonwood, holding his dead son in his arms.

Meade's heart clenched and his pulse throbbed.

He hadn't consciously realized it before, but that image had been plaguing him for hours now, flashing beneath his eyes and sending crickets skittering up his spine.

His rod collapsed completely now. Meade rolled off
the girl and onto his back with an anguished sigh. Breathing hard, he lay his arm across his forehead and stared at
the ceiling. The girl sat up, swung her legs to the floor.

"Maybe shootin' Drake set you on edge," she said,
not looking at him. "I reckon killin' somebody right
before—"

"Shut up and pour me a drink and get the hell out of
here. Any word of this, I'll cut your tongue out and wear
it around my neck."

When the girl had grabbed her clothes and left, Meade
stole out of bed, swept the gauzy curtains aside with the
hand that held his drink, and peered through the window.
The yard was quiet, the barns and corrals dark, only one
light in the bunkhouse. The only movement came from
the horses in the corrals and the cottonwood looming
over the pump house.

"Shit," Meade cursed himself. Disgusted by his own
anxiety, he crept back to the bed, reclined against the
headboard, crossed his ankles, and sipped his drink.

In the room to his left, Running Bear and a girl were
grunting and sighing, the girl muttering, "Oh, honey! Oh,
honey!" and making the bedsprings sing.

Hawk would follow. But only after he'd suffered considerably over his son's grisly murder. That's what
Meade had wanted, wasn't it? Hawk would come, even-
tually, and Meade and his men would kill him. Simple as
that.

Why then did Ned feel as though he were lying naked
in a room full of crazy, murderous savages, his heart
clenched like a tight knot in his chest?

There it was again—the image of Gideon Hawk

standing atop that rain-swept butte, beneath the tree, his dead son in his arms. Somehow, Meade's imagination had doctored the memory so that Hawk's eyes were the red of the devil's in a feverish child's nightmare.

Meade blinked and shook his head, purging his brain of the image. Again cursing himself, he tossed back his brandy, got out of bed, stalked over to the dresser, and poured another. He tossed that one back, set the glass on the dresser. He padded back to bed, drew the sheet and quilt over his naked body, punched his pillow, and lay on his back.

Next door, Running Bear was chuckling and the girl was giggling.

Meade rapped his elbow against the wall. "Pipe down over there, goddamnit. I'm trying to sleep!"

The girl made a shushing sound. The Indian offered one last, muffled chuckle; then all was silent but the breeze wheezing under the eaves and distant murmurs in other parts of the sprawling house.

Meade took several slow, even breaths, and closed his eyes. He felt himself drift gently off to sleep, like a small bird swept away by a warm spring breeze. Meade's mouth opened. A long, thin snore bubbled up from his throat.

An hour passed.

Meade's eyes snapped open. He lay very still, listening.

Outside, a horse whinnied.

Meade grabbed his pistol from the holster and cartridge belt coiled around the bedpost, and swung his feet to the floor. He tramped to the window, crouched, and swept the curtain aside with the pistol.

Across the hoof-pocked yard halved by twin trail ribbons, a shadow flitted along the barn. The barn's big left door opened so slightly as to be nearly unnoticeable. The shadow slipped inside. The door closed behind it.

Breathing heavily, blood rushing through his veins, Meade quickly set his pistol on the dresser, slipped into his pants, shirt, and boots, and buckled his cartridge belt around his untucked shirttails. He slipped out of the room and, walking on the balls of his feet and extending the revolver out before him, felt his way downstairs and out the front door, leaving the door unlatched behind him.

On the porch, he dropped to a crouch and steadied himself with his left hand on the rail, looking around, listening. He gripped the revolver tightly in his right hand. Hawk could have the place surrounded, with one or two men in the barn. Meade had good ears, though, and he heard nothing but the crickets and the breeze ruffling the moonlit willows and cottonwoods rising up behind the barn and the bunkhouse.

It would be just like Hawk to ride solo, to want to take Meade down alone. The lawman could be waiting in the barn for first light, possibly to ambush Meade and his men on their way to saddle their horses.

As if to validate the possibility, a horse nickered—a thin, hollow sound within the barn's stout, log walls.

Meade considered rousting his men. But what if he was mistaken? What if the shadow he'd seen had been only some harmless grub-liner or one of the wranglers kicked out of the bunkhouse for snoring? Meade's imagination might have gotten away from him, and if the boys found out, they might think he'd lost his pluck. Very dangerous—your men thinking you've lost your pluck.

Deciding to take this bull by the horns, Meade bolted off the porch and ran, crouching, across the yard. He pressed his back to the barn wall, left of the closed doors, and listened. Nothing. He reached for the metal handle, pulled the left door open about a foot, and slipped inside. Pulling the door closed behind him, he stepped to the right, staring into the heavy darkness smelling of sour ground blankets and ammonia.

When his eyes had adjusted as much as they were going to, and he could make out the vague outlines of square-hewn ceiling joists and rope stalls, he crept down the alley, one step at a time, swinging his cocked revolver from left to right and back again. He stopped when he heard the soft crunch of straw from straight ahead and to the right. There was a soft shushing sound.

Meade hunkered down on his haunches. Keeping the revolver raised in his right hand, he swept his left across the floor, finding the cool iron of a horseshoe leaning against a stall. He hefted the horseshoe, rose up in a crouch, and heaved the shoe across the barn. It hit the back wall with a solid thud, followed quickly by another thud and a ping as it hit the hard-packed earthen floor.

A horse whinnied. A man yelled something unintelligible—a guttural, startled shout. A shadow moved before Meade. The gunman snapped the Remy up, taking hasty aim and firing four quick rounds. The horse screamed and kicked its stall, raising a thunder nearly as loud as Meade's revolver.

In the gun flashes, Meade saw another shadow move to the right of the first. Swinging the gun that way, Meade emptied the cylinder, the barks resounding, clapping Ned's ears like open-handed slaps.

The first two slugs plunked into flesh, the last into wood.

The horse screamed and kicked—a huge shadow lunging and rearing ahead and left of Meade's position.

Meade stepped quickly to his left and crouched low, automatically flipping open the loading gate, punching out the spent shells, and replacing them with fresh from his belt. The reloading took no more than ten seconds, and when Meade had shut the gate, he realized he hadn't heard another peep from anyone but the horse, the screams of which had settled to angry snorts and nickers.

No more shadows moved.

In the flashes from his pistol, he'd spied a lamp hanging from a post. Now he slid the lantern from its nail, and was fishing around in his pants for a lucifer when alarmed Chinese voices rose from the direction of the bunkhouse, followed by the quick thuds of bare, running feet.

Queen Victoria yelled in a sleepy-froggy voice, "You boys stay right where you are. I'll take care of this." The feet stopped. Something solid was rammed against the barn door three times in quick succession. "What in the hell is going on in there?" the woman yelled.

"It's all right, Victoria—it's Ned Meade."

He was fumbling with the lantern, trying to get it lit, when both doors swung wide. A lantern was thrust at him, an orange glow radiating over the straw-strewn floor, tack-trimmed posts, and dusty stall partitions. Meade turned to see Queen Victoria striding in beneath the raised lantern, wearing men's long underwear and white socks under an open, lemon-yellow night cape while holding a sawed-off shotgun straight out in her right hand. A hairnet covered her tight, blond curls. Several short, stocky figures in smocks flanked the stout woman—her Chinese wranglers and swampers spilling out around her to see what the shooting was about.

The madam had been pushed to the breaking point; her voice was shrill. "Ned Meade, just what on earth do you think you're doing *shooting up my barn*?"

"Give me that," Meade said, grabbing the lantern from the woman's hand.

He raised the lantern above his head as he moved forward down the barn alley, sliding the light along before him. The wan luminescence found a pair of bare, copper-colored feet. It crept up a pair of hairless, copper-colored legs to a limp, glistening dong curled up in a thatch of black pubic hair. It moved up a firm belly and chest with two bullet holes gushing blood.

Meade raised the lantern still higher, until the shadows slid up away from the head of a young Indian with long hair fanned out on the floor beneath him.

Two round holes shone in the buck's forehead, one beside the other, both trickling blood into the wide-open eyes. Blood and brains stained the wall over the body and streaked the young man's hair. The tongue protruding from the buck's thick, cracked lips flicked snakelike several times, then slid to one corner and stilled.

Behind Meade, Queen Victoria clucked.

As Ned moved right, sliding the lantern along above his head, the light revealed the girl he'd taken to bed earlier. She lay sprawled in a low hay mound, half her left temple blown away. But for shoes, black net stockings, and pink feathers in her hair, she was as naked as the day she was born. Both shoes were still twitching.

Feeling stupid, wanting to crawl into a hole somewhere, Meade glanced sheepishly at Queen Victoria, who
shunted her shocked gaze between the two bodies.
"What . . . what in the *world*?" she trilled in her husky
man's voice.

The Chinese were chattering like chipmunks, pointing
at the two bodies on the floor and shaking their heads. A
tall man pushed through them until Lucius Running
Bear's pocked face and bare, fleshy chest appeared in the
lantern light. "Ned, what the hell . . . ?"

Meade thrust the lantern at Queen Victoria, who took
it vacantly, then pushed through the chattering Chinamen
toward the doors.

"Reckon the bitch won't be hornswogglin' me again,"
he grumbled, holstering his .45, splitting the doors, and
heading for the house.

6.

THE DWARF

G IDEON Hawk plucked a .44 shell from the red hand-kerchief spread upon the rough wooden table, and slid the shell through his Colt Army's loading gate, seating the cartridge firmly within its chamber.

He turned the cylinder, let it click on a new chamber, then slid another shell firmly into place. He plucked another shell from the handkerchief and repeated the process.

When the gun had six in the wheel, Hawk sipped from his whiskey glass, then took a long drag from his cigarette. He punched the shells out, one by one, and returned them to the handkerchief, casings down, lead slugs aimed at the low kitchen ceiling across which the light from the hanging lantern flickered.

Night darkened the window over the sink and in the door to the backyard. No stars shone. The wind had died. It wasn't raining but more clouds had moved in, threatening another spring downpour.

The showers had abated just in time to bury young Jubal Hawk yesterday afternoon, in the Shepherd's Hill Cemetery south of Crossroads. Not far from the creek in which the boy had fished summer afternoons with his father for perch and bullheads. There had been a large crowd. Most of the county had shown up, young and old, even some Indians and two doves from the hotel, and paid their respects at the house afterward.

Meats, casseroles, salads, and desserts were spread across the range and countertops. A pie and a quart jar of pickled eggs sat on the table before Hawk—untouched.

Hawk had eaten maybe two bites since his son's death. Linda hadn't eaten a thing.

Hawk refilled his glass from the Old Crow bottle and drank half of it. He plucked his cigarette from the ashtray, drew deeply, and exhaled smoke into the lantern light. He replaced the quirley in the ashtray beside the gun-oil can, and plucked a bullet off the handkerchief.

Holding the shell between his thumb and index finger, he studied it thoughtfully. He was about to thumb it through the revolver's loading gate when a door latch clicked.

Hawk swung his head to the right. Doc Kramer stepped out of Gideon and Linda's bedroom and drew the door shut behind him. Tall and gaunt, with a receding hairline and a stethoscope hanging around his neck, the doctor walked into the kitchen and set his black medical kit on a chair to Hawk's left.

Hawk stared up at him, the lantern light emphasizing the heavy, dark circles beneath Gideon's pale-blue eyes. "How is she, Doc?"

"Well, I finally got her settled down." Kramer sighed

as he removed the stethoscope, wound it up, and stuffed it in his kit. "Took two packages of sleeping powder *besides* the injection I gave her earlier. She's in a lot of anguish. Let's hope she sees her way out of it soon."

"What can I do?"

"Stay with her. Be gentle. Try to get her to eat something when she wakes up, if it's only a piece of bread and some coffee. I'll check on her again in the morning." Kramer reached behind the door, removed his black coat from a hook, shrugged into it, then donned his bullet-crowned black hat. "How're you holding up, Gideon?"

Hawk shrugged and sipped his whiskey. Staring at the bullets lined out on the handkerchief, the lawman said quietly, "I've been shot three times, but I've never felt this miserable, Doc." His hand tightened on the glass, until the knuckles shone white through the sun-browned skin. "Or this much rage."

"Any word from the posse?"

Hawk shook his head.

"Well, go easy on that stuff," Kramer said, pointing at the bottle, a gift from J.T. O'Malley at the hotel. Hawk didn't normally drink at home. "It'll only make it worse."

The doctor turned to walk through the living room to the front door. Hawk started to stand, but the doctor flipped a hand back. "Sit still—I'll see myself out."

When Kramer had gone, Hawk drained his drink, stood, and walked to the closed door of his and Linda's bedroom. He turned the knob and opened the door slightly, peering through the crack.

His young wife slept on her side, beneath two sheets and a quilt with a large, multicolored unicorn sewn into it. Her blond hair lay fanned across the pillow, her eyes

were closed, and her lips were slightly parted and drawn
back, as though even in sleep she were grimacing against
unendurable pain.

At the end of the funeral, when the minister had tossed
dirt onto the simple pine coffin sitting beside the rectan-
gular grave, and said his "ashes to ashes, dust to dust"
prayer, Linda had thrown herself onto the coffin, screaming Jubal's name. It had taken Gideon, J.T. O'Malley, and
Jubal's teacher, Mrs. Craft, to pull her away and lead her
back down the hill to the buggy.

Heavy hoofbeats sounded outside, breaking the
painful memory. Hawk latched the bedroom door, hurried
through the living room, and peered through the picture
window. Riders were streaming toward the house and
bunching up on the street before the picket fence, near the
hitch rack. It was too dark for Hawk to make out their
faces, but it had to be the posse.

Heart pounding, he opened the front door, quickly descended the porch steps, and strode along the brick path
to the gate. All the riders had gathered around the leader,
Emory Tate, Sage County sheriff, who'd ridden over
from St. Joe.

Wearing a thigh-length duck jacket, the lawman stared
down at Hawk from under the brim of his sugar-loaf
sombrero and shook his head. "We tracked 'em as far as
Queen Victoria's. Meade, he killed an Injun up there and
lit out yesterday. The Queen didn't know where they
went and we couldn't cut their sign on account o' the
rain."

"Think the Queen was tellin' the truth?"

"She's never been a friend to the law, but she's
breathin' hornets over Meade's bad manners."

"She say who was ridin' with Ned?"

The sheriff swiped two gloved fingers down his long, gray mustache. "Beaver Face Pyle, Dawson, and the breed, Running Bear."

Hawk stared straight ahead, considering the information.

"We'll get fresh horses and try again tomorrow, Gid."

"No," Hawk said, balling his right fist, trying to keep himself under control. He needed to think through the situation objectively. Going off half-cocked was no way to bring Meade to justice. "They'll be long gone by tomorrow. Best thing to do now is wait for word over the telegraph. Somebody's bound to spot 'em and report it."

When the posse had headed off to the livery barn, their hooves making soft sucking sounds in the still-damp street, Hawk went back inside. He poured himself another drink and paced the living room, thinking. When the living room got too small, he began wandering up and down the hall, then back into the kitchen.

If only he'd gone after Meade earlier, when he'd first seen him under that tree . . .

He sat down and started rolling another cigarette. He'd sprinkled a few grains of tobacco onto the paper when he stopped suddenly and looked up, his pale eyes intensifying as a thought dawned on him.

Mr. Thomas had once ridden with Meade. The dwarf would know where the son of a bitch was heading.

Hawk sat for several moments, then set the paper and tobacco down and peeked again into their bedroom. She lay exactly as she'd lain the last time he'd checked on her.

Finally, he closed the door, went back into the kitchen, and lifted his gun belt off a hook behind the outside door.

When he'd buckled the gun belt around his lean waist, he slipped the .44 into the holster, donned his hat, grabbed his frock coat and Henry, slipped out the front door, and bent his legs for the livery barn on Main.

"Ralph," he called as he strode down the livery's main alley lit by only one lamp on each end, "I'm takin' my horse."

The portly liveryman, Ralph Anderson, appeared in the narrow doorway to his lean-to sleeping area. The man's thick, sandy hair was mussed and his broad, fair cheeks were red, his colorless eyes sheepish. When Hawk had first entered the barn, he'd heard a woman's voice in the rear. The voice hadn't belonged to Anderson's wife, but to Mrs. Sherman from the feed store.

"Good Lord, at this hour?" the liveryman exclaimed with an irritated scowl.

"Send your wife over to sit with Linda till I get back, will you?"

The liveryman glowered at the lawman, raising his voice and repeating, "Good Lord, *at this hour?*"

Hawk set his rifle down, plucked his saddle off a rack, and stepped into the stall in which his buckskin stood hip-shot, eyeing its owner expectantly. He glanced at the liveryman, looked away, then looked sharply back at the man.

As he flung his saddle blanket over the buckskin's back, he said, "But first you better button your pants and wipe that clown paint off your cheek."

Hawk rode west from Crossroads, taking the stage road for four miles, then swinging north on a ranch trail for two. The night was flannel dark, with clouds covering the moon and the smell of wet earth and sage still freshening the air.

Swinging back west, Hawk rode another two miles and reined the buckskin south, until Mr. Thomas's Place appeared on a dark hill, a tall, black rectangle with two pinpricks of yellow light marking windows.

Hawk booted his horse forward, down a sloping prairie hogback, and into a cottonwood grove at the bottom. He dismounted, tied the horse, shucked his Henry repeater, and followed a shallow gully up the next hill.

At the low ridge, he squatted, peered up at the tall house at the crest of the next hill. Two sashed windows in the second story were lit, but Hawk couldn't see any movement within.

Hearing nothing, seeing no movement outside, Hawk walked up the hill, moving slowly, holding the repeater down low in his right hand. He brushed past the single-hole privy, wincing at the cloying, pungent odor of human waste—Mr. Thomas needed to move the damn thing—then traced a curving path through the sage and rabbit bush to the house's back door.

Muffled voices rose from the second story, as well as intermittent wooden thumps.

Hawk turned to the door, jerked the leather-and-metal latch. Locked. It wasn't much of a lock. Hawk plucked his double-edged bowie knife from the belt sheath on his left hip, jammed the knife between the door and the frame, drew it sharply up.

The lock broke, part of it falling and hitting the inside floor with a rattling thump.

Hawk froze. Upstairs, the muffled voices and occasional thumps continued.

Hawk sheathed his knife and, swinging the plank door wide, raised his rifle in both hands, stole up the two wobbly brick steps and over the threshold. He'd been to Mr. Thomas's Place enough times to know the layout; in spite of the inner darkness, he made his way to the stairs on the left side of the cluttered main room, moving slowly to avoid bumping into shelving racks and tripping over junk.

An indignant cat gave him a momentary start, and then he was on the stairs, taking the steps two at a time, walking on the balls of his feet. A half minute later he stood in the second-floor hall, partially lit by the lamplight spilling out the quarter-open door before him.

He rammed the rifle butt against the door, popping it wide, then stepping into the room, using his right boot to catch the door on its way back to the frame. He began raising the Henry, but checked himself.

Before him, Mr. Thomas's naked wife was down on all fours, facing the window. Mr. Thomas, naked except for a red neckerchief, broad-brimmed, high-peaked hat, and black, child-sized cowboy boots, stood behind the moaning woman, thrusting his naked hips. His pale, hairy legs bent and straightened, bent and straightened, as the dwarf tugged on the belt he'd looped over the woman's neck.

"Come on, Stretch. Give me a whinny, damn ye! Give me a whinny!"

Gagging, the woman lifted her head and gave a sort of strangled whinny. Her face was bright red, and sweat ran in beads down her cheeks.

Mr. Thomas drew his head back, laughing and thrusting. Doing so, he caught a glimpse of Hawk filling the room's doorway, rifle raised to the lawman's shoulder.

The dwarf froze and released the belt. The woman dropped with a groan.

Mr. Thomas turned toward Hawk, sweating and flushed, eyes wide and red-rimmed. "How'd you get in here, you son of a bitch?"

Rifle raised and aimed, Hawk moved toward him. The dwarf wheeled to grab his gun off the bed behind him. When he turned back toward Hawk, Gideon thrust the Henry's barrel through Mr. Thomas's gritted teeth.

Mr. Thomas's hand, and the gun it held, stayed on the bed. The dwarf's head slammed back against the brass frame. He gagged and grabbed the barrel of the Henry with his left hand, but Hawk's grip remained firm, pinning the dwarf's head between two brass rods in the frame.

The woman swung a terrified look over her shoulder, then scampered over to the wall, put her back to it, and raised her knees, wrapping her long arms around them to hide her breasts. The woman shunted her horrified gaze from Hawk to Mr. Thomas and back again, her anvil jaw hanging. The belt was still looped around her neck.

"B-bastard!" she cried. Hawk wasn't sure whom she was addressing—him or Mr. Thomas. He didn't care.

To Mr. Thomas, he said through gritted teeth, "You're the only one low enough in this whole county to tell Meade about my son."

The dwarf's mouth opened around the rifle barrel. "Gunghghrrrr."

"Now, you're gonna tell *me* where ole Three Fingers is headed."

"Unhhhgunghrrrrr!"

"Or I'm gonna blow your brains out."

From the wall, the woman shrieked, "You l-leave Mr. Thomas alone, you son of a b-bitch!"

"Shut up," Hawk said quietly without looking at her.

He removed the Henry's barrel from the dwarf's mouth.

Mr. Thomas swallowed and shook his head to clear it, then stared up at Hawk beseechingly. "You crazy bastard! I'm an American. I got unalien rights!"

Hawk glowered down at him, inched the barrel toward his mouth. The dwarf looked at the rifle.

"I don't know!"

Hawk stared down at the small, naked man. He didn't blink.

"Honest to St. Christopher, you big bastard. He never told me!"

The lawman's shoulders slumped, and he let the rifle barrel drop. He could always tell when Mr. Thomas was lying, because the dwarf's right eye drifted slightly inward, toward his long, hawkish nose. Now, both pupils stared up at Hawk, and straight ahead.

Hawk stood where he was for nearly a minute, glaring into the dwarf's beady eyes. Finally, he turned and walked slowly to the door. Stopping, he turned his head slightly. "When I've got Ned, I'll be back to shut you down."

He moved forward and down the dark stairwell. Behind him, he heard the big blonde sobbing and cooing, "There, there, Mr. Thomas. You're all right n-now."

"Big bastard!" Mr. Thomas shouted, his voice cracking with fury. "I've got unalien rights!"

*   *   *

An hour later, Hawk returned to his house. Dora Anderson, knitting in his rocker under a smoking lamp, reported that Linda hadn't stirred all the while he'd been gone.

When Dora had left, Hawk checked on his wife. She was in the same position he'd left her in, curled beneath the colorful unicorn quilt. Quietly latching the bedroom door, he blew out the lamps, kicked his boots off, and lay down on the sofa, beneath the trophy head of the pronghorn buck he'd shot last fall.

It took him two hours to fall asleep.

When he again opened his eyes, morning light flooded the room. He stomped into his boots, shuffled into the kitchen, started a fire in the range, and set a percolator to boil.

Gently rotating his head to work the knots from his neck, he tapped on the bedroom door. When Linda didn't answer, he opened the door and peered into the room.

The bed was empty, the sheets and unicorn quilt thrown back upon themselves. Hawk stepped into the room, raking his gaze from left to right.

"Linda!" he called.

As he was about to turn and leave the room, something in the window caught his eye. He strode to the sashed pane, swept the lace curtains aside, and cast his glance into the backyard.

Hawk stumbled back against the bed, as if pushed by an unseen hand.

Outside, a sprawling box elder stood right of the old buggy shed with rotten shake shingles. From a stout limb of the box elder hung a body with long, golden-blond hair and wearing a nightgown and cream-colored robe. The robe buffeted like angel's wings. The pale, bare feet turned slowly in the easy morning breeze.

The rope from Jubal's tree swing was knotted around Linda's twisted neck.

7

HAPPY TIMES

THREE months later, Ken Dawson, Lucius Running Bear, and Beaver Face Pyle rode through the foothills of a nameless desert mountain range. They descended a bench studded with saguaros and scrub yucca, and started across the playa stretched upon the desert floor below.

The sun beat down relentlessly, reflecting off the cracked, white plain. The horses kicked the fetid alkali up into the sweating riders' faces. On the hot, dry air, the thick, sickly-sweet fetor of a dead coyote wafted. Right of the trail, the remains of the animal's rib cage showed through the picked, sun-bleached hide, the skull lying intact at the end of the exposed vertebrae.

The tin, five-pointed stars on the men's shirts and vests winked in the harsh light. Those reflections were all the man watching from the distant town could see—the bright, intermittent flashes and vague, ant-sized silhouettes of three riders swimming through an oceanic heat-haze.

On the playa, Running Bear lifted his blue bandanna over his pitted, cherry-red cheeks and nose and glanced at Dawson. "What'd that telegram say again?"

Dawson glanced back at him, irritation in his eyes. He plucked a pink telegraph flimsy from his shirt pocket and thrust it over to the big Indian riding the tall Appaloosa on his left. "I done told you 'bout twenty times now. Read it for yourself."

"You know I can't read, you uppity son of a bitch."

Dawson stared at him hard. "That's *Sheriff* Dawson to you. Don't forget that, Lucius."

"Oh, for chrissakes," said Beaver Face Pyle, riding on the other side of Dawson. "I'll read it to him."

Dawson held the Indian's stare for five more seconds, then turned and thrust the note out to Pyle, who took it in his gloved hands. Holding the flimsy out before him as his horse plodded along beside Dawson's, Pyle lifted his voice dramatically and read, "Meet me in Rio Concepción. Stop. Noon tomorrow. Stop. To discuss a certain boy and the upcoming election in Silver Lode. Stop."

Running Bear stared over Dawson's steeldust gelding at Beaver Face Pyle, the big Indian's black eyes squinted with incredulity. "You mean to tell me that's all it says? Nothin' about who wrote it or about where *exactly* to meet the son of a bitch?"

"Lucius, a man who never took the time to learn how to read should be a little more trusting of those of us who did."

"Kiss my ass, you beaver-faced ferret!"

Pyle's face swelled with anger. He opened his mouth

to speak, but before he could say anything, Dawson said, "Shut up and start actin' professional—both of you! You're supposed to be my deputies. Lawmen do not, I repeat, *do not* fight amongst themselves!" He whipped his head around to each man in turn.

They stared back at him angrily, then gradually, looking cowed, turned away.

When Dawson saw that he'd successfully quashed the argument, he rode, quietly brooding, for several yards, going over the telegraph again in his own mind.

"I have a feelin'," he said as the town grew out of the heat-haze before them, "that whoever this hombre is will find *us*. He's probably even got his eyes on us right now."

"What do you s'pose he wants?" Running Bear asked, running his gaze along the handful of brick adobes, stock corrals, and windmills strewn about the chaparral a hundred yards ahead, at the foot of a long, bald rimrock stretching northeast to southwest.

"Blackmail, no doubt," Pyle speculated, wincing against the sun and fishing a stubby tobacco braid from his shirt.

"What's blackmail?" Running Bear asked. "I heard but I forget."

The burly menace in Running Bear's voice, coupled with Dawson's reprimand, kept Pyle from offering little but a disgusted grunt.

Dawson explained, "He knows what we done with Ned up in Crossroads, and he's gonna try to get money out of us, or blow the whistle on us up in Silver Lode. If we lose the election, MacGregor ain't gonna like it . . . after all the work he's done to get us elected."

"How we gonna play it, Kenny?" Pyle said.

Dawson laughed without humor. "How do you think? We're gonna kill him! And if there's more than one, we're gonna kill 'em *all*. It'll be easy—hell, we're the law in this county!"

Dawson booted his horse into a lope. Five minutes later, he, Running Bear, and Pyle crossed the thin stream trickling through cottonwoods, pushed their way through the half-dozen goats grazing in the shade along the water, and rode into town.

They pulled up at the white adobe livery stable on the town's northeast end.

"Amigo, I have a question for you," Dawson said to the man carrying a forkful of hay and manure through the barn's gaping doors. The wiry old codger in a ratty straw sombrero dumped the load into a cart hitched to a hang-headed donkey aswarm with flies. "I'm Sheriff Dawson from Silver Lode. We have come to see a—"

Without turning to Dawson, the old man pointed to a long adobe building sitting diagonally across the wide, dusty street, with a front patio shaded by a brush arbor. A sign nailed over the roof read HAPPY TIMES in big, block letters. On the patio were several wooden tables and benches. Before one of the two hitch racks out front, a black barb stood, hip-shot, the sun glistening on the mount's rich coat. The rifle boot mounted over the horse's right shoulder was empty.

"Grain and water our horses," Dawson ordered the old man, sizing up the place across the street and shucking his Winchester from his saddle boot. "We shouldn't be long."

"*Sí, sí.*"

When Running Bear and Pyle had slipped their own ri-

fles from their scabbards, they set out after Dawson angling toward the cantina. Stepping over clumps of fresh
horse plop, the men strode single file past the barb and
onto the patio, where bluebottle flies buzzed over the
spilled beer and food scraps on the rough wooden tables.
A liver-colored puss sat hunched over one of the beer
spills. Hearing the strangers, it swung its head toward
them. One eye was gone, leaving a pinkish bald scar over
the socket. Its single eye intensifying, the cat whined and
leapt to the floor, then up and over the stone wall in a
blur.

On the other side of the patio, Dawson mounted the
two steps to the cantina's main entrance and stopped, his
rifle held across his chest. Running Bear and Pyle waited
behind him, canting their heads to peer around him, rising up on their boots to see over him.

Dawson blinked and squinted into the shadows, his vision slowly adjusting, clarifying the long plank bar to the
left, the dozen or so tables scattered across the hard
earthen floor. The room was broken up by square ceiling
joists from which tangy-smelling *ristras* of chilis and
jerked beef hung. A faro layout and bullet-scarred piano
were against the far left wall.

A short, bald man stood behind the bar, peering at
Dawson and fingering his long, yellowing mustache
speculatively. Dawson stepped into the saloon, Pyle and
Running Bear following, all wielding rifles. The man
cleared his throat, seemed about to say something, then,
muttering nervously, turned and shuffled through a narrow door behind the bar. The door slammed behind him.
A latch was thrown with a click.

Dawson stood in the middle of the room. Pyle flanked

him on his right, Running Bear on his left. The three men moved forward, toward a table on the far side of the room.

A man sat behind the table. He leaned back casually in his chair, which was pulled sideways, an elbow on the tabletop. A whiskey bottle stood near his arm. Light from the window revealed the label: Old Crow.

Near the man's right hand lay an ashtray in which a cigarette smoldered, the gray-blue smoke rising in slow, even curls toward the ceiling. Behind him, an arched window revealed a view of the trail Dawson and the others had taken into town. No doubt the man had watched them travel down from the mountains and across the playa.

"You got us here," Dawson said, stopping six feet in front of the table, Running Bear and Pyle walking up on either side. "What the hell you want?"

The man studied him from beneath the low crown of a black Plainsman—a dark-featured hombre, ever so vaguely Indian, with lake-green eyes and long, auburn hair curling over his ears. His high, broad cheeks were shadowed by his hat brim and by a three-day growth of brown beard stubble. He wore a dusty frock over a white, silk shirt and fawn vest, a watch chain drooping from the vest's right pocket.

The man's eyes bored so deeply into Dawson's that Dawson felt as though they were raking his very soul. Vaguely, he wondered if he should recognize the man. He'd never seen Gideon Hawk up close, but he'd heard he was big and dark-haired, that his mother had been a Norwegian immigrant, his father a Ute.

Was this Hawk?

Blood pounded in Dawson's ears. His edginess turned to anger. He squeezed the rifle in his hands. "I just asked you—"

"Congratulations on the new job," the stranger said softly. "You're comin' up in the world, Ken."

"Who the fuck are you, mister?" Running Bear barked, nostrils flaring.

The stranger looked at him without expression, then casually slid his gaze back to Dawson. "Where's Ned?"

Dawson opened and closed his hands around the rifle and again took the measure of the man before him. Damn calm son of a bitch. Cool as trail apples in January. "None of your business where Ned is. Said in your telegram you wanted to discuss the election. Well, say what you got to say."

"I don't want to discuss the election," the stranger said. "I just said that to get you over here, away from that crooked town and that crooked council that hired you after they killed the sitting sheriff last month." The stranger studied Dawson, and nodded once. "I know about MacGregor and his plans to take over the county, fleece the miners and cattlemen. I know about it, and for the moment, I don't care. MacGregor can wait."

Dawson canted a look at Pyle standing on his right. Frowning, he turned back to the stranger, but despite his sour guts and the blood pounding in his ears, he didn't say anything. He'd wait for the stranger to show his hand.

The man leaned farther back in his chair, glanced casually out the window, folded his hands across his vest, and drew a deep breath through his nose. "And I don't care, for the moment, to discuss the boy you murdered up in Crossroads, either."

The man's eyes darkened suddenly, the heavy lids sliding down a quarter inch as the pupils expanded. "That, too, can wait for another time and another place. All I want right now from you three is Ned Meade."

No one said anything for a full half minute. The stranger sat staring up at Dawson. Dawson, Pyle, and Running Bear stared down at the stranger.

"Why, you're Hawk," said Pyle, his voice low-pitched with anxiety.

Hawk didn't look at him. Fingers laced on his vest, he swallowed down the dry knot in his throat and kept his eyes on Dawson. "You boys give me Ned, and you can turn around and walk out of here. Free as sparrows. You don't give me Ned, I'm taking you in . . . to hang."

Pyle turned to Dawson and pointed at the lawman. "Why, that's Gideon Hawk."

"Shut up, Beaver Face," said Lucius Running Bear, peeling his lips back from his gritted teeth and regarding Gideon Hawk flinty-eyed, his big chest rising and falling sharply.

"Don't do anything stupid," Hawk said slowly, inching his left hand down toward the stag-butted Army Colt on his hip. "Just tell me where you last saw Ned."

Ken Dawson stepped back slowly, his breathing growing erratic. "Where we last seen Ned?" he stalled.

"Yeah, that's right."

Running Bear stood where he was, but Pyle skitter-stepped sideways and back, his face flushing so red that the whites of his eyes stood out like pearls. He was breathing hard, his hands leaving sweat streaks on his Spencer carbine.

His gaze raking them, seeing what was coming, Hawk said softly, "Don't do it."

He'd barely got the last word out when Beaver Face dropped his Spencer's barrel, thumbing the hammer back. The rifle swung toward Hawk. Hawk raised his right hand, jerked the wrist slide, which smoothly deposited a double-barreled, pearl-handled derringer into his palm. His index finger slid through the trigger guard while his thumb brought one of the two hammers back.

The peashooter popped a half second before Pyle triggered his Spencer, whistling a bullet past Hawk's left ear and into the wall behind him. Pyle groaned and dropped the Spencer as Hawk's .36-caliber slug tore through his belly. He was dropping to his knees when Hawk, seeing that Running Bear was lowering his Winchester a shade faster than Dawson was bringing his own weapon to bear, jerked the pistol toward the big Indian and fired.

The round ricocheted off the Indian's rifle receiver, shattering and spraying fragments into the man's face and neck. A big chunk buried itself in his shirt just over his heart. Running Bear made a face, as though he'd just eaten a sour apple. He stumbled backward, dropping his rifle and bringing his hands to his face.

"Fuck! Goddamnit. Fuck!"

Meanwhile, Dawson triggered two rounds in quick succession, both slugs plunking into the thick adobe wall as Hawk bolted forward out of his chair. The lawman hit the floor on his left shoulder and raised his Colt as, turning with him, Dawson jacked another round into his rifle's chamber and fired.

The shot plunked into the floor just right of Hawk's face. The lawman triggered his big Colt, loosing four rounds in quick succession, drilling Dawson low in his right side, in his left shoulder, in his left arm, and through the right edge of his neck.

Screaming and clutching his rifle, Dawson spun, dropped to one knee, bolted forward, and ran toward the front door. He dropped again, still screaming. As the rifle clattered to the floor, he fell to his hands.

Hawk heaved himself to his feet. On his knees, lips stretched back from his buck teeth, Pyle picked up his rifle and aimed at Hawk, who now held his big Russian as well as the Colt. The pistols barked simultaneously, drilling two neat holes through Beaver Face's forehead. Pyle's head snapped back on his shoulders. He groaned and gurgled and flapped his arms, like an earthbound bird trying to coax himself into flight.

Hawk snapped his gaze to Running Bear.

The Indian had gained his knees and brought his rifle to his right shoulder. He snugged his bloody face to the stock and fired.

Hawk dove onto a table, which broke beneath his weight. As he hit the floor with a crash, the Indian's rifle spoke again. The bullet seared Hawk's left shoulder. The lawman scrambled to his feet and crouched behind a sheet-iron brazier.

The Indian bounced lead off the brazier, shouting, "You're gonna die, Hawk!"

Hawk raised both pistols and fired. Levering another round into his rifle's breech, Running Bear ducked at the last instant. Hawk's rounds flew on past the Indian and parted the hair of Dawson crawling toward the door behind him.

Running Bear's voice boomed off the walls. "You're
going where your kid went, lawman!"

Hawk crouched down behind the brazier, dropped the
empty Colt, and took the Russian in his right hand.

The Indian's voice rose in volume as the man staggered toward the brazier, chuckling. "I'm gonna do you a
big favor!"

Hawk extended the Russian over the brazier. The raging Indian triggered his rifle. Hawk ducked as the round
clanged and sparked off the iron, spraying the wall behind him with lead fragments.

Hawk extended the pistol over the brazier. The Indian's eyes snapped wide with panic as the .44 popped
twice. Both shots took Running Bear high in the chest,
punching him back against a joist. His rifle hit the ceiling, then landed with a boom as the hammer smacked a
live cartridge.

The slug blew the Indian's lower jaw away in a spray
of red mist. Running Bear slumped to his right shoulder,
shuddering and scissoring his thick legs.

Behind him, Dawson gained a knee and swung his rifle
back behind him one-handed. The rifle barked, geysering
smoke and flames, the slug tearing through Hawk's right
sleeve and burning his forearm. As Dawson dropped the
rifle and lunged through the open door, Hawk fired the Russian. Outside, Dawson grunted, grabbed his thigh, and staggered onto the patio.

Walking stiffly, the Russian lowered to his left thigh,
Hawk crossed the room and, ducking under the lintel,
strode through the door and onto the patio. Ahead, Dawson gained the hitch rack. His blood-splattered rifle lay

on the patio tiles. One hand clutching his bloody neck, he jerked at the reins of Hawk's tied barb.

Seeing Hawk in his vision's periphery, he snapped his sweat-streaked face to the lawman. His neck and shirt were blood-soaked. The outlaw cursed, gave up on the reins, and half-ran, half-stumbled down the street.

Hawk walked across the patio and followed Dawson, who stumbled and shuttled looks back behind him, cursing and shouting, "I'm sheriff of Silver Lode County! Someone help!"

No one appeared on either side of the street. In the shop windows, shutters and blinds had been closed. The liveryman had closed his barn doors. Besides Dawson and the lawman dogging his tracks, all that moved on the street were a tumbleweed and a single goat nibbling the high grass along the general store's raised boardwalk.

From a distant chimney wafted the faint, spicy aroma of chili con carne.

"Someone, help me. I'm your sheriff! This crazy son of a bitch is tryin' to kill me!"

Halfway between Hawk and a brick saddlery set off from the other buildings around it, Dawson half-turned to Hawk and dropped to his left knee. He drew his pistol, half-raised it, then, too weak to fire the gun, let it drop to his side.

His head drooped between his shoulders.

Hawk stood over him, staring down.

Dawson glanced up at the lawman and screamed shrilly, "Kill me and get it over with, ye crazy son of a bitch!"

Hawk's chest rose and fell steadily. His ruddy skin was stretched taut across his broad, russet cheekbones. Blood spotted his vest at the nub of his shoulder; it stained his black frock over his right forearm. His lake-green eyes darkened to spruce.

In his mind, he raised the .44 to Dawson's head and pulled the trigger.

He took another deep breath and swallowed the constriction in his chest. "I'm gonna need you alive, Ken." He blinked his eyes clear. "Ken Dawson," he said, his voice taut with official restraint, "you're under arrest for the murder of Jubal Hawk."

8.

SHEPHERD'S HILL

TWO weeks later, Gideon Hawk and two other deputy U.S. marshals—young Luke Morgan and an older man named Bill Campanella, whose right cheek and jaw had been horribly scarred when an outlaw buffalo hunter had thrown molten bullet lead in his face—cantered along Wolf Creek east from Crossroads. They traversed the creek on a narrow wooden bridge and started up a tawny butte toward the stones and crosses of the Shepherd's Hill Cemetery strewn amidst chokecherry shrubs and cottonwood trees.

It was a breezy day on the high prairie, with big puffs of summer clouds obscuring the cerulean sky and shuttling shadows along the hock-high grass. The creek wound along the butte's base, dark green and gently ruffled, sheathed in shrubs and huge, gnarled trees. Carp and bluegill lightly kissed the creek's surface, trolling for mayflies.

Halfway to the butte's crest, Hawk, Campanella, and

Morgan halted their horses under a creaky box elder. Silently, Hawk dismounted from his buckskin, handed his reins to Morgan, then turned and walked along the butte's shoulder. In his left hand he held a clump of lilacs freshly picked from the bush outside his and Linda's bedroom window. In his right hand he carried a small, wooden horse carved by Jubal—one of many that littered the boy's room.

When Hawk came to the two fresh graves sitting side by side, he stopped and stared down. Linda's lay on the left, Jubal's on the right. The two mounds of freshly turned earth were flanked by a single large stone in which Linda and Jubal's names had been carved, along with the dates of their births and deaths. Gideon's name and birth date were there as well, with a space left for the date of his death.

Hawk stared at the graves for several minutes, then dropped to one knee and set the lilacs on the soil mounded over Linda's grave, the horse on that over Jubal's. The breeze slid the lilacs around. Hawk picked up a heavy dirt clod from the base of the mounded soil and set it atop the stems, holding them in place, then adjusted the blossoms into a spray of sorts.

When Hawk had adjusted the horse atop Jubal's grave, so that it appeared to be riding off toward the creek and the vast, cloud-gauzy horizon rolling up beyond, he stood and swept the dirt and grass from his knee. He set his hat on his head, adjusted the angle, and shuttled his gaze between the graves.

"I love you both. See you again soon."

Quickly brushing a tear from his cheek, he turned, walked back over to the horses, and took his reins from

Luke Morgan. He swung up onto the buckskin and adjusted the cross-draw pistols on his hips. "Let's catch a train."

Morgan shared a glance with Campanella.

"Let's do that, Gideon," said Campanella, hard-jawed.

Ken Dawson had told them they'd likely find Meade in Montana, where he'd gone when he'd split up with Dawson, Pyle, and Running Bear—their faces now too familiar to be seen together.

Hawk gigged the buckskin down the butte toward the breeze-frothed creek, Luke Morgan following, the tall, scarred, stiff-backed Campanella bringing up the rear.

Three Fingers Ned Meade rode into a bustling mining camp, threading his way around bull wagons and dead-axle•ore wagons, and reined up before a saloon from which raucous piano music pounded amidst men's laughter and the clatter of roulette wheels.

Meade took a long cautious look around. Seeing no lawmen, he swung down from the saddle, looped his reins over the hitch rack, and mounted the boardwalk. As he stared toward the batwings, a vague figure in the corner of his right eye made him stop suddenly and turn. His head hadn't stopped moving before a tall figure in a black frock, bullet-crowned black hat, and fawn vest withdrew behind a nearby building corner.

Little electric lightning bolts snapped in Meade's arteries. He stepped forward slowly, gunmetal brows knit with deep thought. Instead of moving on into the saloon before him, he turned left and began walking along the boardwalk. He walked neither quickly nor slowly, but kept a moderate pace, arms hanging relaxed at his sides, his right thumb twitching involuntarily toward the Remy on his hip.

When he'd neared the cross street, Meade stopped and turned casually toward the window of a harness shop, as though something in the fly-flecked, dirt-streaked window had caught his eye. He canted his head and rolled his gaze sharply right, until he saw the tall man in the black frock stop suddenly, holding a pistol in each hand, then leap behind a doorway.

Blood pounding, Meade turned and crossed the street, picking up his pace and nearly getting flattened by a lumber dray. He mounted the opposite boardwalk and glanced over his right shoulder. The dray was slowly turning onto the main street, the driver popping his blacksnake over his mules while loudly berating Meade, shaking his free fist.

Ned ignored the skinner, watching instead the man in the black frock leave the opposite boardwalk on the other side of the wagon and jog toward Meade, using the slow-moving wagon for cover.

Just before the wagon swung onto the main street, Meade bolted into a narrow gap between two buildings and drew his revolver. He crouched between the buildings, a foot back from the boardwalk, and waited.

Boots pounded the worn planks. The tall man in the black frock strode swiftly past Meade, eyes straight ahead. Meade waited until the man was on his right, heading on up the street, then stepped onto the board-walk and thumbed back his revolver's hammer.

"Hawk!" Meade shouted.

As Hawk stopped and swung around, bringing his pis-

tols to bear, Meade fired. Grinning, he fired again as
Gideon Hawk dropped his pistols and clutched his chest,
stumbling back and falling in a heap.

"Meade!" someone shouted behind him.

Ned swung around, pistol extended. He blinked his
eyes as if to clear them. The dark-haired, mustachioed
man moving toward him wore a bullet-crowned black
hat and black frock, string tie swirling back behind his
neck. As the man raised the big pistols in his hands,
Meade shot him, then wheeled and ran to the left through
the gap between the buildings.

He was halfway to the buildings' rear when a figure
stepped out from behind the one on the right. "Meade!"
the tall man in the black frock shouted, raising a stag-
butted Colt in one fist, a silver-plated Russian in the
other.

Meade ran to a skidding stop and fired.

"Meade!" a voice boomed behind him.

Ned wheeled in time to see another black-frocked
figure raise two pistols to his face, both barrels yawning
at him like the bell-shaped maw of a blunderbuss, black,
toothless jaws opening to swallow him whole.

"You're dead, ye bastard!"

Someone jerked Meade's shoulder and his eyes
snapped wide as he rose up on his elbows, the wool blanket slipping down his chest. "Ned, wake up!"

Meade blinked.

His heart's pounding slowed.

Sweat dribbled down his gaunt, pasty cheeks. Before
him, Poker Joe Carlysle's face swam into focus. Poker
Joe crouched over Meade, the man's broad, bearded face
bunched with befuddlement and concern. Beyond Joe,

Clayton Ellard leaned back against a river willow and thumbed cartridges through his Schofield's open loading gate. Ellard was grinning, chuckling.

"Get your damn hands off me!" Meade pushed Poker Joe away and threw off his blanket.

Pearl dawn light washed over the camp, where the nine other men of Meade's gang, whom he'd rejoined last night in Ennis, in Montana's lower Madison River Valley, milled around a small, snapping fire, shaving or dressing or hunkered over coffee cups. All were staring at Meade with expressions ranging from curiosity to glee at the outlaw leader's embarrassing display of obvious terror.

"That must've been one hell of a dream, Ned," said Clayton Ellard.

Meade turned his colorless gaze to the outlaw, his heartbeat slowing. "I was dreaming I was shooting your mother, but the old whore wouldn't die." He turned to the others. "Put that fire out and get mounted. We don't have time to sit around drinkin' coffee all morning! We got a bank to rob!"

The others kicked dirt on the fire, and scattered. Ellard was still sitting back against the willow, grinning up at Meade. "You wouldn't have been dreaming about a certain lawman, would you, Ned? Maybe the one whose son you threw a hemp party for?"

Meade stared at him, his expression flat. "Don't get suicidal on me, Clay."

"Ah, hell, Ned, I was just joshin'." Tobacco quid showed through Ellard's greasy grin. Born and bred in Oklahoma, where he was wanted for kidnapping, rape, and murder, Ellard pushed himself to his full six feet four inches and spat. "Shit, when I killed that warden's wife, I dreamt about the warden's boys comin' after me for the next two years. That's why I went back to Knoxville and killed the warden. Right then, the dreams stopped."

"Thanks for the advice," Meade said, keeping a lid on his fury. "Now, shut up and saddle your horse."

Ellard shrugged, reached down, and grabbed his saddle. "Whatever you say, Ned."

When Ellard was gone, Meade crouched to roll his blanket. Cursing under his breath, Ned tied the blanket with rawhide, grabbed his saddle, and moved off toward the horses, making a mental note to kill Ellard as soon as they'd robbed the bank and were heading for Mexico.

He was ten yards from his horse when Hawk's visage flashed up behind his eyes, running toward him along the boardwalk, revolvers spitting smoke. Meade's step faltered. He threw his hand out, steadied himself against a tree.

He looked around at the other riders, silently smoking and saddling their horses in the misty dawn shadows, the Ruby River running silently beyond them, between low, grassy banks. None of the men were looking toward Meade.

Ned shook his head, snapped his eyes open and closed, and moved briskly to his horse.

A half hour later, Meade's gang galloped down from the grassy, pine-spotted foothills of the Gravelly Range. They followed a deep-rutted wagon road through the center of the Gallatin Valley and into the humble little ranching burg of Ennis—little more than a block's length of false-fronted businesses flanked by cabins and shanties and a few two-story brick houses in the cotton-woods down by the river. Despite the town's modest size, the Hereford cattle that Meade had noted peppering the rich, green valley on both sides of the river bespoke a vibrant ranch economy.

The bank midway down the town's main drag—a two-story limestone building boasting a recessed entry, a carved frieze, and heavy oak doors with glass upper panels and brass knobs—supported the assessment. Most banks in this neck of the woods were glorified tents and cabins. The sweat that had muscled this place out of the broom grass and sage had wealth behind it. Eastern wealth, no doubt. Maybe even a few blooded, moneyed Brits had discovered the spruce-green Gallatin grass nurtured by chuckling creeks and roaring rivers.

Meade's mouth watered at the prospect of the paper money and gold specie no doubt tucked away in the bank's stony shadows.

Poker Joe Carlysle must have been sensing Meade's thoughts. Riding off Ned's right stirrup, Poker Joe said softly, just above the clomping of the gang's horses in the dusty street, "We done been here the past three weeks, and this place is a friggin' gold mine, Ned. Rich ranchers movin' in, stowin' their money away in the stockmen's yonder. Here's the popper. The only law here is one old man—a broken-down ex-Texas Ranger—and his deputy, the tinhorn son of a stockman. Word is the stockman thinks his son is the next Bat Masterson, only the kid can't shoot fer beans, and the half-breed railroad hunters come to town every Saturday night and kick the holy shit out of him."

Poker Joe lightly punched Meade's shoulder and snorted a laugh. Meade glanced at his shoulder, then at Poker Joe. Ned didn't smile. Sobering, Poker Joe cleared his throat.

"Anyway, this here little burg's our El Dorado, Ned. I swear on a stack of Bibles. Why—"

"That's enough, Joe," Meade said, reining his horse toward the Gallatin Saloon, sitting on the left side of the street, kitty-corner from the bank. "You're gettin' over-wrought. Very unattractive."

"Sorry, Ned."

Meade and the others dismounted and tied their horses to the three hitch racks fronting the broad, clapboard-sided saloon. Meade turned, gave the bank another quick study. He removed his bowler hat, ran his hands through his stringy, white hair. He turned his close-set eyes to Jimpson and Morales, who were already watching him, awaiting his nod.

Meade nodded.

The plan was for Jimpson and Morales to go over to the jailhouse and take care of the lawmen as quietly as possible, then meet Meade and the rest of the gang in the Gallatin. From there, the gang would walk across the street and tend to their banking.

When Jimpson and Morales had drifted on down the street, Meade stepped onto the boardwalk before the saloon. As the other eight men pushed through the batwings and into the cool shadows beyond, Meade stopped suddenly, whipped his gaze to the right.

Had a frock-coated figure just bolted into that gap be-tween the millinery and the bathhouse?

Meade's pulse quickened, then slowed. Christ, he needed to get out of this country before there was noth-ing left of his nerves but fine, frazzled hairs.

He pushed through the batwings and ordered a rye.

9.

ENNIS

STANDING alone at the bar, Meade threw back the rye and ordered another. The other men had ordered shots, then taken seats at two tables. According to plan, so they wouldn't pique the suspicion of the bartender and the single, smiling dove playing solitaire at a table near the bottom of the stairs, the men broke out the pasteboards and started a blackjack game.

Ned threw back the second rye and set the shot glass on the zinc bar top. Polishing the mirror over the backbar, the apron turned to Meade, one eyebrow cocked in question.

Meade shook his head. "As a man of temperance, I allow myself only two before noon."

The bartender nodded and went back to work on the mirror.

Meade was about to sit down with the other boys, who were working a little too hard at enjoying their card game and not thinking about the bank money and the señoritas

down Mexico way. Jimpson and Morales pushed through
the batwings. Morales sat down near the cardplayers, as
if to observe, while Jimpson sidled up to Meade.

"They weren't there," the stoop-shouldered Jimpson
said, lighting a quirley while pretending to watch the card
game with interest. "Door was open, coffee was even on
the stove"—Jimpson shook his head and blew out the lucifer—"but the law wasn't there. Didn't see 'em on the
street, neither."

Meade stared at the men tossing cards around the table
and thought it over. A chill crawled up from between his
butt cheeks. He couldn't rely on that, though. These days,
a loud bird or sudden dog's bark was enough to get his
blood pumping. You couldn't call off a long-planned
bank job just because a couple of tinhorn badge-toters
weren't where he'd expected they'd be. They could have
been called out to see about long-loopers. Hell, they
could be in one of the town's two other saloons, oiling
their tonsils or playing slap and tickle with the local
sporting girls.

Meade cleared his throat.

The others fell instantly silent and looked up at him.

Meade nodded.

When the others had nonchalantly gathered their
cards, finished their drinks, mashed out their cigarettes,
and sauntered out the doors, Meade glanced at the bartender. The man was regarding him curiously, fingering
an end of his waxed mustache. Meade glanced at the
whore. She regarded him as well, her card deck held in
one hand, a single card in the other. She wasn't smiling
anymore.

Meade smiled at them both, pinched his hat brim, turned, and strode through the batwings.

The others had gathered on the boardwalk, lined out abreast and facing the street. Meade stepped between Poker Joe and Roy Morales. He took a breath, then moved to his horse, reached inside a saddlebag for a roll of burlap sacks, and tossed them to several of the other men, who stuffed them inside their coats.

"Let's go."

Meade and the gang left the boardwalk, filtered through their horses tied to the hitch racks, and angled across the street. They paused to pinch their hat brims at two ladies—a mother and daughter, it appeared, clad crisply in checked gingham dresses, with capes and poke bonnets—passing in a dusty black buggy with high, red wheels. When the buggy had passed, the women nodding curtly, the men continued to the boardwalk fronting the bank.

Two gang members took up positions on either side of the front doors while the others filed inside behind Meade. When the last man had gone inside, the door closed.

The SORRY—CLOSED sign was turned to face the street, and the shades were drawn.

The men guarding the door stood there as if they'd only stopped to chat, but instead of chatting, they raked their gazes up and down the street, still quiet this time of the day. Most of the noise was made by a yapping yellow dog tied to a post before the blacksmith shop at the other end of the business district.

The two men outside the bank were grateful for the dog. Its yaps covered the yelling and occasional screams and whimpers from inside the bank. There were no pistol shots. Meade didn't usually have to kill anyone if he yelled loudly enough, which scared everyone inside the bank half to death.

Not five minutes after the gang had gone in, the doors opened suddenly and the men filed out, nearly all clutching moneybags in their fists. A few were grinning.

They paused outside the bank, looking around. Meade asked the men he'd left outside if they'd spotted any trouble.

"Not a thing."

"Easy as opening a peach tin," said Poker Joe.

"Let's go," Meade said, stepping off the boardwalk and beginning to angle back across the street, toward the horses tied to the hitch rack before the Gallatin.

Before he'd taken three steps, he stopped. Ahead, boots thumped and spurs chinged. Men were filing out of the saloon. Well-dressed men, sporting the moon-and-star badges of deputy U.S. marshals. Most wore mustaches. A few had graying hair, but most appeared in their twenties or early thirties. They all carried rifles.

Moving almost casually, all eight filed off the boardwalk, stepping between the hitch racks and the horses and into the street, lining out abreast in the street before the saloon.

Just as they'd all gotten settled, movement in the balcony over the boardwalk attracted Meade's eye.

The balcony door had opened, the glass flashing sunlight. An old man with a huge gray mustache and wearing a five-pointed sheriff's star stepped outside, clutching a double-barreled Greener in his thick, brown hands.

Behind him came a tall young man with a long, thin nose and close-set eyes beneath the down-angled brim of a black sugar-loaf sombrero. He, too, carried a shotgun. The star on his fawn-skin vest flashed in the wan morning sunlight. He wore two pistols, butt-forward and low, like a *pistolero*.

"Well, I'll be god*damned*," Meade heard Poker Joe exclaim softly to his right.

"How do you want to do this, Ned?" The third lawman from the left had spoken.

Meade looked at him. There was a hard knob in his chest and his throat pulsed. The lawman stepped out from the others—a tall man in a black frock, with a fawn-colored wool vest, a black string tie, and a flat-brimmed black hat. Clear green eyes fairly sparkled in the golden sunlight beneath the hat brim. A dark brown mustache folded down around the man's wide mouth.

Gideon Hawk was a good inch or two taller than the tallest of the others. He wore a stag-butted Colt on his left hip, a silver-plated Russian on his right, butts tilted toward his belt buckle for easy access. In his big hands he held a brass-framed Henry repeater across his chest, his right thumb resting lightly on the hammer. A thin gold wedding band shone on his ring finger.

Meade peered into those emerald-green eyes. His heart had been pounding. Now, it slowed. A strange calm settled over him. He managed a half smile. "Hawk."

"You and your gang are under arrest, Ned. Drop your weapons and stand down."

Meade dropped the two moneybags in his hands. Around him, the other men did the same. "The odds are almost even, I'd say," Meade said. "Even with those two tinhorns in the balcony."

The clatter of wagon wheels rose in the west. Meade turned. The buggy and the two women were heading back through town. The women were arguing, turned to each other instead of the street ahead of them.

"Nancy, I told you . . ." The rest of the older woman's sentence was drowned by the breeze, the yipping dog, and the clatter of the buggy's wheels.

Hawk saw the buggy, too. He saw the cunning glint in Meade's eyes. He squeezed his rifle and took another step forward. "Throw 'em down, Ned. I won't tell you again."

Meade's eyes shifted again to the buggy. Hawk mentally urged the woman to stop, but she seemed oblivious to everything but her argument with her daughter . . . something about a dress pattern. The men around Meade were flushed with excitement, shifting their eyes quickly from Meade to the approaching buggy to the lawmen facing them on the other side of the street.

Their hands hung beside their pistols. Many were flexing, twitching . . .

Hawk didn't look at the other deputy U.S. marshals around him, but he could feel their tension.

The buggy was fifteen yards away. Ten . . . "Nancy, you know we can't afford all that ribbon and lace. You should be ashamed for such frivolous notions!"

From the balcony above and behind Hawk, Sheriff Milt Cory shouted, "Mrs. Hostetler, for godsakes, turn that buggy around and get the hell *outta here*!"

Meade's thin lips stretched a grin. Hawk shot a quick glance at the buggy. The older woman had fallen silent and snapped her head forward, frowning with curiosity.

The paint kept moving along the street, puffing its lips and twitching its ears suspiciously.

"Mother . . ." the daughter warned.

Hawk had no sooner turned back to Meade than Meade slapped leather. His pistol was out in a flash. It barked, geysering smoke and flames. Hawk had crouched at the last instant, and the bullet smacked into the awning support behind him.

Dropping to one knee, Hawk raised the Henry and fired two quick shots, both slugs plunking street dirt behind Meade's heels as the outlaw, bone-white hair flying out from his bowler, sprinted toward the carriage. In seconds, Meade darted past the horse, and by then, all hell was breaking loose as the outlaws began slinging lead at the lawmen.

Hawk swung the Henry right and cut down on two men cutting down on him, their slugs buzzing past him on both sides and shattering the saloon's front window. Hawk drilled one man through the right shin while the other was taken out by Bill Campanella standing off Hawk's right elbow.

Hawk was too concerned about Meade for accurate shooting at the other outlaws. The older woman screamed as Meade, climbing aboard, shoved her aside and grabbed the reins of the nervously prancing paint. Several outlaws had gathered behind Meade, ducked behind the horse and buggy, using the carriage as a shield.

From the balcony above Meade, the old sheriff shouted, "Stand down, you greasy sons o' whores!"

The shotgun exploded, rocking the street as it echoed off the bank. Two outlaws returned fire. The sheriff groaned. Hawk heard the wooden railing break and saw, in the corner of his left eye, a figure fall and hit the street with a thump, lost amid the popping rifles and revolvers and the horses' terrified whinnies.

At the same time, Meade, crouched atop the buggy, slapped the reins and yelled, "Mooooove, ye mangy beast!" As the horse lunged off its hind feet, the older woman screamed again as she tumbled over her daughter, turned a somersault off the buggy's right rear wheel, and hit the street in a pile of green-checked gingham.

"Momma!" the girl screamed, thrown back in her seat as the buggy bolted off behind the fear-addled paint.

Hawk raised his rifle, wanting desperately to snap off a shot at Meade. Knowing he could hit the girl, he shot instead at one of the outlaws facing him through the dust of the departed buggy.

As his shot swung the man around and threw him back against the hitch rack fronting the bank, his gaze raked five outlaws slumped or stretched flat in the dirt, blood glistening. One man—whom Hawk recognized from a wanted dodger as Clayton Ellard—groaned and lifted his hatless head to peer at the bullet hole just above and right of his groin.

Just as quickly, Hawk glanced around his side of the street.

Three of his own men were down, one with a bloody hole in his temple. The sheriff lay ten feet to Hawk's right, chest rising and falling, but the several holes in his chest would doubtless claim him soon. The other marshals were either on their knees or crouched behind stock troughs, returning the fire of the outlaws shooting from building corners.

Dust and smoke sifted as guns popped. The dog had

fallen silent. In the balcony above Hawk, the sheriff's young deputy choked out anguished groans. East along the street, the wagon careened around a corner and disappeared.

"I'm going after Meade!" Hawk yelled, and wheeled toward the hitch rack where the outlaws had tied their mounts.

One horse lay in a bloody heap while two others crow-hopped and jerked at their ties. The others had pulled loose and scattered.

Hawk swept a dun's reins from the rack, leapt into the leather, and spurred the horse through the buggy's still-sifting dust. He whipped the reins against the horse's neck, urging more speed as he followed the main drag's slow curve to the right.

The two-story businesses, clapboard houses, and outlying shanties rushed past. Then he was beyond the town, following the wagon road through meadows splashed with wildflowers and shaded by occasional cottonwoods, the Gallatin River flowing, lilac-blue and sun-scaled, along the low buttes on his right.

Hawk hunkered low over the lunging dun's whipping mane. Ahead, the buggy appeared, climbing a low hill stippled with cedars and sage clumps.

Hawk whipped the reins against the dun's neck and stabbed his spurs into its loins. Just behind his eyes, Jubal appeared, hanging from the cottonwood in the wind-blown rain. The boy's boots kicked as his legs spasmed, dying even as Hawk galloped up the hill toward the tree.

Linda . . . hanging from Jubal's tree swing . . . head canted toward her shoulder . . . wide, staring eyes reflecting the morning sun . . .

The preacher's words: "The cold injustice of such a brutal act leaves us stunned and questioning God's charity, as does a mother's stygian grief. I can offer few suitable explanations for such horrors, only assure you that the men who took young Jubal long before his time, and drove his grief-stricken mother to take her own life in the wake of her child's passing, will pay for their transgressions. . . ."

Hawk ground his jaws, blinked, and shook his head, clearing the words and the images.

Ahead, the buggy grew so that he could pick out Ned and the girl from the black seats. The girl sat to Meade's right, flopping back against the seat, tawny hair blowing in the wind. Meade stood, crouching, whipping the reins against the galloping paint's broad back. The outlaw's white hair and the tails of his checked coat streamed out behind him.

Meade shot a look over his right shoulder and through his hair streaming like corn silk across his mouth. Seeing Hawk, he stretched a grin, slipped his revolver from his holster. The gun smoked a quarter second before the pop reached Hawk's ears.

The lawman flinched as the bullet smacked a tree on his right, snapping a branch. Hawk touched his holster, but he couldn't return fire and risk hitting the girl, a fact of which Meade was very much aware.

He had to get closer . . . without getting shot . . .

Again, he ground his heels into the dun's sides and crouched low in the saddle. Meade snapped off two more shots, one bullet singing over Hawk's right shoulder, the other yelping off a rock just behind him. Ahead, the buggy rose up and over the hill's crest, sun-gilded dust rising.

A quarter minute later, Hawk and the dun leapt over

the hill. Halfway down the other side, Meade had turned the buggy left to miss four horseback riders climbing the hill in a loose group—drovers, by their dusty trail garb. The riders were reining back on their own mounts and yelling warnings as the buggy swung off the trail. The girl screamed as the carriage rose first onto its left wheels, then its right. It slammed back down onto all four wheels as the paint raced across the meadow.

"Rein 'im in, fool!" shouted one of the cowboys.

"Where's the race?" yelled another.

Hawk swung the dun into the meadow after the bouncing buggy. He'd galloped maybe twenty yards before the buggy's left wheels dropped into a shallow gully. As the runaway paint jerked the wheels back out, the buggy caromed sharply left, and rolled.

Meade and the girl flew like rag dolls in high arcs through the sparkling mountain air. The girl landed first. Two seconds later, Meade landed several yards beyond her. The paint pulled the toppled buggy off across the meadow, shaking its head as it made a beeline for a distant cottonwood grove.

Hawk dismounted on the run and crouched beside the girl. She was rolling onto her back, shaking her head and blinking her brown eyes groggily. "You all right, miss?"

The girl looked around, as if not quite sure where she was. When she mumbled that she thought she was all right, and Hawk had seen no bones were broken, he walked toward Meade.

The outlaw lay at the lip of another shallow gully, his right leg awkwardly bent, no doubt broken in several places. The outlaw groaned and regarded Hawk through the stringy hair splayed over his eyes. Meade's revolver was nowhere in sight.

Hawk stood over the man and stared stiffly down.

Meade groaned and hissed through his teeth, "I'm gonna need a doctor, Hawk. Oh, Jesus, my leg's broken!"

Hawk blinked, drew a deep breath through his nose. In his mind's eye, Meade was sitting atop the hill, beside young Jubal hanging from the cottonwood branch. The outlaw lifted his arm, waved in a broad arc.

Hawk thumbed back the hammer of the revolver in his right hand hanging straight down at his side.

Behind him, hooves thudded. He did not turn to look as the drovers rode toward him, or as Deputy Luke Morgan approached on a galloping roan. Morgan split the group of drovers, rode past the girl, who sat gathering her faculties, and checked his mount down to a trot. As he approached Hawk and Meade, the deputy dismounted and sidled up to Hawk. He held a pistol in his right hand.

Meade cursed and begged for a doctor.

"Doctor, hell!" Morgan spat.

He crouched over Meade, jammed his pistol into the man's mouth, forced his head back to the ground. Meade's eyes snapped wide, his dark, scaly face a Halloween mask of horror. He choked and gagged, kicked his good leg.

"Want me to do it, Gid?" Morgan asked. "He deserves it, sure enough."

Hawk's string tie whipped back across his shoulder, and his chestnut hair slid around in the wind. His coat lapels flapped. Slowly, he depressed the Colt's hammer, returned the pistol to its holster.

His voice was low and brittle. "Cuff him, Deputy."

10

RED DUCK AND PORTER

THE marshals had lost five men, including the sheriff and his young deputy, but the only outlaw left alive was Ned Meade. Hawk and Luke Morgan hauled Meade back to Yankton, where the killer was hospitalized until he was well enough to stand trial.

Hawk waited around Yankton, dealing faro, until it was his turn to testify at Meade's trial. To a hushed courtroom, Hawk gave his testimony simply and officially, then strode out of the room, out of the courthouse, across the street, and into the Cattleman's Saloon, where he chased two quick shots with a beer.

Two days later, cattle rustlers killed a ranch family north of Fort Pierre, on the Cheyenne River, and he volunteered to go after them, wiring Luke Morgan in Bismarck to meet him at the Rock Creek Stage Station along the Missouri River. Having also robbed a mail coach, the rustlers were wanted on federal warrants.

Hawk saw no reason to wait around for the jury's verdict. The evidence was incontrovertible. Justice would be served. He had to move on with his life despite how hollow it felt without Linda and Jubal.

He picked up the rustlers' trail at the burned ranch and followed it north, leaving instructions at the Rock Creek Stage Station for Morgan to follow. On the afternoon of his fifth day of pursuit, after he'd spooked the rustlers off the herd they'd been moving toward Canada, the tracks vanished suddenly at a ridge base not far from Bear Den Creek.

Hawk reined his buckskin up suddenly, and stared uphill at the jumbled mass of boulders and the gold aspens rising toward a blue-marble sky. The tracks vanished amongst the flat granite boulders.

A faint warning bell tolled in his ears. There'd been no need for the rustlers to leave the valley for the ridge he faced now, unless they knew he was still trailing them and had decided to remedy the situation once and for all. His right hand strayed to the holster on his left hip, released the keeper thong over the Colt. On the breeze came the faint, barely recognizable tang of wood smoke.

The warning bell tolled louder.

Hawk had just reined his horse left, booting the animal hard, when a slug buzzed through the air where his chest had been a half second before, and spanged off a rock behind him with an angry *pee-yinngggggg!*

As his startled buckskin bucked, Hawk leapt from the leather, grabbing his Henry from the saddle boot and fluidly throwing himself back away from the horse's flailing hooves. The riderless horse galloped back down the hill. Rolling behind the boulders, Hawk levered a shell into the rifle's breech, rose up onto his left hip and shoulder, and peered through a six-inch gap between the rocks.

Silence. Thirty yards ahead, the aspen leaves shook, glinting gold, in the breeze.

Hawk rose onto his knees, then bolted left, diving past a six-foot gap in the boulders. As he hit the ground on his elbows, a rifle popped, the heavy-caliber slug plowing up sod and leaves and echoing like massive drumbeats along the hillside.

Hawk rose to his knees again and peered over the boulders. In the tangled chokecherry scrub beside an aspen bole twenty yards up the hill and to the right, gray smoke wafted. Sunlight glinted off the blue steel of a rifle barrel.

Hawk rammed his Henry through the gap in the boulders and dusted five quick shots, squinting through the smoke and flames leaping from the rifle's maw. The bullets beat the shrubs, chewing up leaves and branches. The shots hadn't ceased echoing before Hawk heard a thump, like something solid hitting the ground. There was a low, guttural curse.

"U.S. marshal!" Hawk shouted. "You're under arrest." He rammed another shell into the Henry's chamber, his anvil jaws set hard on both sides of his mustache.

A loud, venomous curse rose from the shrubs. "You killed me, you son of a bitch!" The strain in the man's voice told Hawk it wasn't a trap.

The lawman crawled over the boulders and, holding his rifle in one hand, climbed the hill, skirting the chokecherry scrub to come at it from uphill. He shoved aside an aspen branch with his rifle barrel and peered into the gold-edged shadows of the undergrowth, where a big man sat propped against an aspen bole. He had a three-day growth of beard on his broad, angular face, and wide-set eyes. He'd lost his hat, and his pewter-gray hair was sweat-matted to his head.

He was facing downhill and south and did not turn to look at Hawk. "Of all the lousy goddamn luck," said James Frank Boggs. Hawk recognized him from his wanted dodger. Wanted for cattle rustling in Arizona, and for that and more here in Dakota Territory.

Hawk stepped toward him. Blood and gore puddled the man's middle, just above his belt buckle. His right leg was bloody in two places. His big Sharps '50 lay straight ahead of him in the torn branches. "Keep that hand away from your shoulder holster."

Boggs grunted and shook his head balefully. "I had you in my sights a few minutes ago, woulda killed you good, but just as I was takin' up the slack in my trigger finger, big goddamn garter snake slithers across my boot. Gives me a start and I look away. Hate snakes. When I turn back to you, you're bootin' your horse toward the rocks." The man chuckled, then winced at the pain. "Musta missed you by four inches."

"Your camp smoke gave you away."

"Shit, I doused it ten minutes ago. Just wanted a little coffee while I waited. You must have a good nose."

Hawk glanced around, uphill and down, keeping his Henry trained on the dying Boggs. "Where're the others?"

The man shook his head.

"They left you to dust me off your back trail," Hawk said.

The man held his guts with both hands. "Goddamn snake," he muttered.

"Where'd they go?" Hawk asked.

The man said nothing, just stared straight ahead as if pondering the mercurial nature of fate.

Hawk stepped forward, crouched, and removed the Smith & Wesson from the man's shoulder holster. He tossed it into the brush. "You don't owe them a thing, Boggs. They left you here to die."

The man stared, thinking it over. Woodenly, the light slowly leaving his eyes, he said, "South. Saloon . . . Bear Den Crossing." A faint, malign smile tugged at his mouth. "Marty's gotta . . . girl . . ." He fell straight over on a shoulder. His shoulders rose and fell, a foot shook, then the body stilled.

Hawk stared down at him, slowly lowered his Henry. He took the rifle in his left hand, raised the gloved right one to his face. In the past, lead swaps had gotten his blood pumping, made him shaky. Not so much afraid for himself as for Linda and Jubal, leaving them alone.

The hand he stared at now, however, could have been stone. His heart seemed to barely be pumping.

He turned and walked away through the brush.

Two hours later, Hawk rode up a long, sloping grade toward a ridge covered with long grass and peppered with burr oaks and ironwood. Behind him, Boggs's horse, a skittish, doubtless stolen, black Morgan, followed on a lead rope, the outlaw's body tied belly-down across his saddle and covered with his soogan.

Hawk crested the ridge, stared down at the motley collection of shacks gathered along Bear Den Creek, then clucked to the buckskin and rode lazily down the hill, and reined up before the saloon and hotel—a two-story building painted barn-red and sporting a second-story balcony with a white rail.

Hawk dismounted, tied both his horses to the hitch rack, and loosened their cinches. As he stepped around behind the Morgan, he ran his eyes across the five other horses tied to the rack.

Three standing stirrup-to-stirrup were dusty and sweat-lathered. The rifles had been removed from their saddle boots.

Hawk shucked his own Henry, levered a shell into the breech, and off-cocked the hammer. Sometimes the best approach was the direct approach. His spurs chinging on the scarred puncheons, carrying his rifle in his right hand, he mounted the raised boardwalk and pushed through the batwings.

Moving quickly toward the bar on the room's right side, he ran his gaze quickly over the tables on his left, instantly picking out two of the three men he was looking for—two dusty hard cases lounging at one table near the piano, several empty shot glasses and beer mugs strewn before them. Trouble was, between Hawk and the hard cases were a couple of farmers and three drovers playing faro with a skinny gent with gold-frame glasses and a green eyeshade. Two more men, miners in low-heeled, lace-up boots and plug hats, played cribbage for matchsticks at the room's rear.

Too many innocent bystanders for Hawk to risk a lead swap here on the saloon's main floor. He'd have to lure them either outside or upstairs. Since the third man was probably upstairs . . .

The bartender was the bored, friendly sort who wanted to chat. Hawk waved off the portly gent's banter and

asked for a room upstairs, glancing at the two dusty hard
cases in the mirror behind the bar.

The two rustlers watched him intently, disbeliev-
ingly—a tall, red-haired gent with short hair in a battered
black hat and brown batwing chaps, and a chubby kid
with long black hair, tattoos on both beefy arms, two pistols in shoulder holsters, and a big bowie sheathed on his
chest, between the pistol butts.

The barman frowned. "A room?"

Hawk nodded.

The fat man beetled his thin, sandy eyebrows. "Kind
of early for turnin' in, ain't it?"

"How much?"

"One dollar for the night. My girl's busy at the moment, but if you want company . . ."

Hawk glanced at the mirror. The third gent was probably with the girl. Hawk looked at the bartender. "Just the
room."

When he'd slapped a dollar on the bar top and scooped
up the key, he glanced once more at the two outlaws in
the mirror. They were shuttling exasperated gazes between him and each other. He turned, walked along the
bar to the back of the room, and stepped through the door
standing open beside an empty whiskey keg. He closed
the door behind him, and climbed the stairs.

Hawk's boots on the stairs behind the closed doors
were the only sound in the saloon for several seconds
after he'd left. The outlaws turned their heads from the
closed door to each other, their eyes bright from drink
and exasperation.

The men scraped their chairs back, stood, grabbed
their rifles from across a nearby chair, and walked to the

batwings. They stood staring over the batwings for several seconds before, side by side, they pushed out onto the boardwalk and approached the Morgan over which their dead partner was draped.

Flies hovered over the horse, like a dust cloud.

The redhead, Quinn Porter, handed his rifle to the beefy kid, Ramon Red Duck. Porter raised the mouse-chewed blanket from the dead man's head, revealing the pewter hair. Grabbing a fistful of hair, Porter lifted the head, revealing Boggs's bearded face, eyes tightly shut, chalky lips stretching a grimace.

Porter released the head, which slapped the Morgan's ribs, and looked at Red Duck. They stared at each other, eyes blazing.

"Take the back," Porter said, grabbing his rifle back from his partner and jacking a shell into the Henry's breech.

Without a word, Ramon Red Duck raised his own rifle high, turned, mounted the boardwalk, and strode swiftly around the saloon's southeast corner.

Upstairs, Gideon Hawk strode down the narrow corridor lit by the single window at the end of the hall. Hearing the whine of bedsprings and the sighs of lovemaking, he stopped before Room 7, stepped back, raised his right foot, and slammed his heel against the door, just left of the knob.

The door exploded inward, showering splinters from the frame, revealing a bed to the right, a bearded black man and a tawny-haired woman toiling beneath the sheets. Hawk strode forward, using his rifle butt to knock the ricocheting door back against the wall, and stopped a foot from the bed as a framed tintype crashed to the floor.

He raised the Henry to his shoulder and aimed at the man lying atop the woman. The man had turned to him, mouth agape, black eyes furious. Beneath him, the woman stared at the rifle, transfixed.

"Deputy U.S. marshal." With his left hand, Hawk reached behind him, unhooked his handcuffs from his cartridge belt, and dangled them before the black man. "Put 'em on—you're under arrest."

When he had gagged the black man and cuffed him to the bed frame, and hidden the tawny-haired girl in the closet, he jacked another shell into his Henry's breech and sidled up to the door frame. He stretched a glance through the frame, looked leftward along the hall, then right, toward the stairs, where a loose board squeaked beneath the musty carpet runner.

With another leftward glance, Hawk sidled down the hall toward the stairs, holding his rifle in both hands and keeping his back to the wall.

Five feet from the top step, he stopped. He waited, breathing slowly. When he'd taken three breaths, another stair board creaked and a low-crowned hat appeared along the left side of the staircase, the brim tipped back to reveal the redhead's freckled face and wide, brown eyes.

Locking eyes with Hawk, Quinn Porter stiffened and froze.

"No need to die," Hawk said reasonably. "Just drop the rifle and raise your hands."

A second stretched. The redhead's eyes flicked to Hawk's left, as if glancing at something back along the hall. The man crouched and raised his Henry. Gideon dropped his own Henry's forestock to his left hand and shot the redhead twice, the ejected shells bouncing off the wall and rolling down the steps with tinny clatters.

As the man screamed and slammed against the wall behind him, Hawk turned sharply left.

The dark, tattooed kid had him dead to rights, a Spencer rifle aimed directly at Hawk's head.

Behind the half-breed, a gun spoke. Blood and brains erupted from the kid's right temple. He twisted sharply right as his own rifle geysered smoke and flames, the slug blasting into the wall just over Hawk's right shoulder, shattering a bracket lamp.

The half-breed dropped to his knees, his Spencer clattering to the carpet. At the other end of the hall, smoking pistol extended, silhouetted by the bright window behind him, stood Deputy Luke Morgan.

"The other one dead?" he asked.

Hawk glanced down the stairs. The redhead lay on the saloon floor, just beyond the open door, in a growing pool of blood, one leg curled beneath the other. The bartender and the other customers stood around him, glancing from the body to Hawk at the top of the stairs.

Hawk nodded, depressed his Henry's hammer, and lowered the rifle to his side. Turning, he moved toward the room in which he'd cuffed the black man. Morgan met him at the door, frowning.

"Should've waited for me, Gid. You almost got drilled."

Hawk shrugged and turned into the room. The young deputy grabbed his right arm. "A telegram came for you in Bismarck."

Hawk turned to the young man sporting a thin red mustache and curly red sideburns. Morgan wore a broad-brimmed hat like Hawk's and a blue silk neckerchief, dust-coated from his hard ride from Bismarck. He shoved a pink telegraph flimsy at Hawk.

Hawk glanced at the flimsy with mild annoyance. "What's it say?"

"It's from Broyles." Pete Broyles was the head marshal out of Yankton. "The county attorney said we arrested Ned Meade illegally."

Hawk glared at Morgan.

"He declared a mistrial and released him." The young deputy swallowed. His voice quaked. "Gideon, Ned's *free.*"

11

PARKS

HAWK let Luke Morgan clean up the mess at Bear Den Crossing while Gideon raced back to Yankton.

The big lawman learned from an assistant in the stone county courthouse on the banks of the broad Missouri River that the prosecuting attorney, Benton T. Parks, had released Ned Meade "due to lack of physical evidence and reliable eyewitnesses."

His fists grinding into the assistant's oak desk, eyes pinning the young man to the back of his chair like a fly to the wall, Hawk said, "You sayin' the body of my dead son wasn't *enough*? *My testimony* wasn't *enough*?"

Nearby, another clerk stopped playing his typewriter and turned to stare, wary-eyed.

The young man with pomaded hair parted in the middle stared up at Hawk, his brown eyes behind the glinting spectacles big as mule shoes. "That's what Mr. Parks said, Mr. Hawk. I had nothing to do with it."

"The judge agreed to this?"

"On the recommendation of Mr. Parks, he did, sir. Mr. Parks already submitted his brief to the Department of Justice in Washington, sir."

Hawk glanced at the closed oak door bearing a plaque gold-engraved with Parks's name. He straightened and started for the door.

The assistant cleared his throat and croaked, "Mr. Parks isn't in, Mr. Hawk."

Hawk stopped. "Where is he?"

"H-he and Judge Newcomb went fishing. They'll be out of the office until day after tomorrow."

Hawk's eyes slitted and his cheeks dimpled. "Ain't that handy." He took a deep breath, resisting the urge to tear the room apart and pummel the haughty-eyed assistants with his fists. "You tell him when he gets back that he and I'll be having a talk. In the meantime, I want a copy of that brief. Send it over to Lucille Inger's Boarding House."

Hawk slammed the door behind him and descended the broad, marble stairs to the ground floor. His head swirled and his heart beat heavily as he thought through the two-pronged problem of Meade's release from prison and the man who released him. The law had been getting more and more complicated every year, but there was no way in heaven or hell Parks or anyone else could justify the release of Ned Meade. Someone in Meade's camp had to have gotten to the prosecuting attorney, either threatened him or bribed him.

Standing in the courthouse's front doorway and peering into the street below the broad, stone steps, Hawk absently fished a match from his coat pocket, stuck it in his mouth, and chewed.

Which man would he go after first?

Meade was no doubt feeling pretty smug. He shouldn't be too hard to find. Give him a few days to enjoy his freedom and let his guard down.

Parks, on the other hand, was probably feeling a little nervous. Nervous men made mistakes. Might as well cook while the pan's still hot. Hawk would stick around Yankton for a while, look into the doings of Mr. Benton T. Parks, uncover his obviously illegal associations, and throw the bastard in the same cell from which he'd sprung Three Fingers Ned.

Deep in thought, Hawk strode down the steps and mounted his horse. He was heading down a cross street when soft, insistent cackling sounded on his right, barely penetrating his consciousness. Hawk had ridden on past the laughter before he realized the voice sounded familiar. He swung a look behind him.

On the corner stood a sprawling, two-story general supply store casting shade onto the side street where several wagons and saddle horses milled. On the store's raised, roofed loading dock, the despicable, ubiquitous dwarf, Mr. Thomas, lowered a twenty-pound sack of flour to the big blonde he called Stretch, who turned and set the bag into the box of a heavy-duty buckboard.

Mr. Thomas straightened when he saw Hawk. He flashed a broad grin under the brim of his boy-sized straw hat thonged snugly beneath his chin and scraggly goat beard. Chuckling and rising up on the balls of his boy's black boots, he raised a pudgy hand to his hat, saluting. "Mr. Hawk, how lovely to see you."

Hawk sighed. Mr. Thomas obviously had something to say. Since the dwarf's big mouth had proven useful in the past, Hawk reined the horse around and put him up to the boardwalk.

"Top o' the day to you, Marshal! Me and the missus just come to town to fill the larder."

Hawk glanced at the woman standing at the back of the wagon, gloved hands hanging at her sides, returning Hawk's gaze dully. She wore a man's checkered shirt and blue jeans, her lusterless, straw-yellow hair swirling down from her floppy-brimmed hat, framing her flat face and dumb, close-set eyes.

Turning back to Mr. Thomas, Hawk said, "Something tickle your funny bone?"

The dwarf gave his head a delighted wag. "I was just thinkin' of ole Ned Meade. Why, he's slipperier than a snake dipped in honey!"

"I know Ned's free. Chew it up a little finer and spit it out."

The dwarf feigned a pained expression, giving his overlarge head another wag. "Damn shame what ole Ned did to your boy. Did I hear wrong, or did your grief-stricken wife kill herself only one night later?"

Hawk stared at the bellicose man, jaws clamped.

"The boy *and* his mother dead. Man, did your luck drop in the shitter!" Mr. Thomas threw his head back and rose up on his toes, guffawing. "Couldn't have happened to a nicer fella!"

"Obliged for your sympathy. Right touching."

Laughing, the dwarf danced a quick little jig atop the loading dock, his diminutive heels clattering atop the scarred boards. He finished with a macabre pirouette, landing on both feet, facing the street, throwing his arms out and his head back, laughing with unfettered delight.

Stretch looked up at her husband dully, as though so accustomed to such behavior it no longer had the power to evoke a response.

Hawk wanted to draw his revolver and shoot the little man-dog through his bulging forehead, but he kept his right hand on his thigh, just above his knee, his fingers digging into his twill trousers. His face was a stone mask.

With an ironic arch of his brow, he said, "Mr. Thomas, I'd bet credits to navy beans you know the story behind Ned's flight to freedom."

"I know everything, Marshal. You fail to appreciate that."

"Suppose you share it with me."

"Why should I?"

"'Cause you want to so bad that your shriveled-up little heart is going to explode if you don't."

The dwarf laughed again, but there was no humor in it. He glanced at the tall, blond woman shuttling her uneasy gaze between him and Hawk. "Listen to that bullshit, Stretch. Can you believe how he just talked to me?"

The woman just kept shuttling her glance back and forth between the two men, like a deaf-mute.

The dwarf glared down at Hawk. Although he was standing atop the loading ramp, his head was only a foot or so higher than the lawman's. Hawk held the little man's gaze, sensing the bizarre workings behind those beady eyes.

Finally, Mr. Thomas jerked his child's overalls up his bandy thighs and squatted down on his haunches. He hooked a finger, beckoning Hawk closer. When the lawman gigged the buckskin up beside the loading dock, the dwarf leaned toward him.

Hawk smelled the cheap liquor on his breath, and something else. Malted milk balls?

"Ned's cousin, Dayton Priest, sent three private detectives up here to sniff around Parks. They found out the bastard has a mistress—dance-hall singer named Delia Montgomery—and gambling debts up the wrong end. Followin' me so far?"

Hawk stared at the dwarf skeptically, trying hard to not recoil from the fetid breath washing over his face. He glanced over the roof of the courthouse on the other side of Laurel Avenue, at Benton Parks's gaudy, two-story Victorian mansion perched atop the river bluffs beyond.

A wagon trail curled up the bluffs to the Victorian's front yard, the twin tracks ablaze in the late-day sun. It was public knowledge that Parks's wife, Lydia, had been bedridden with consumption for the past three years.

If knowledge of Parks's mistress became known—if there really *was* a mistress and Hawk wasn't being hornswoggled by the man-carp squatting before him— Parks's political career and reputation would be ruined. He'd have no way of providing for his sick wife, or paying off his gambling notes. Parks would leave his ailing wife destitute. Parks himself would probably end up living in the river buttes with the prairie dogs.

Hawk said, "They blackmailed him?"

The dwarf nodded. "Darn tootin'. And offered him a gold bar from a train held up down Arizony way. The gold was the cherry on top."

Hawk stared at the man skeptically, his mouth a hard line beneath his mustache.

Mr. Thomas curled his lip, grinning. "You don't believe me?"

"No."

"See for yourself. Come Friday, he's due to fetch the gold bar Meade and Grey's boys hid somewhere in the countryside."

"Where?"

Mr. Thomas shrugged and growled wickedly, "Maybe I don't know *everything*."

Hawk stared into the dwarf's eyes, wondering if the man was telling the truth. Parks had prosecuted many of the owlhoots Hawk had hauled back to federal court for trial. Gideon had gambled with the man a time or two, and while he wouldn't call Parks a friend, he knew Parks's professional reputation as an upright public servant.

Would Parks have succumbed to blackmail, releasing a cold-blooded killer like Three Fingers Ned Meade?

Hawk scrutinized Mr. Thomas, who grinned at him like a kid waiting for a jelly bean. Hawk had been a thorn in the dwarf's side for several years, destroying his stills and foiling his attempts to sell liquor to the reservation Indians. Mr. Thomas could merely be trying to lure Hawk into the countryside to dry gulch him under cover of darkness.

"Why are you being so accommodating all of a sudden?" Hawk asked, producing a cigar from his shirt pocket and biting off the end. "We ain't been exactly *close*."

"Ain't that the gospel," the dwarf said, eyes suddenly hard. "Call it Parks's comeuppance, for throwin' me in the pen for stealin' hay I never stole. Anyone as two-faced as him, uppity on one side, crooked-dirty on the other, deserves to spend some time with a few of the men he put away."

Hawk looked off, thoughtful, then lit his cigar and returned his gaze to Mr. Thomas. "Where'd Ned go?" Hawk asked, exhaling a long smoke plume. "Where might I find this cousin of Ned's, this Dayton Priest?"

"If I told you that," the dwarf said, giving a thin, cunning smile, "I might as well tie an anvil around my neck and throw myself in the river. Now, if you'll excuse me and Stretch, we got work to do."

Sucking thoughtfully on his cigar, Hawk headed for the boardinghouse, where he'd rent a room until Friday.

12.

JUDGE LYNCH

FRIDAY night, Gideon Hawk rode the buckskin around behind Laurel Avenue, then dismounted and led the horse up through a gap between the McCormick Opera House and the Palomino Saloon and Dance Hall, and watched Laurel Avenue from the shadows.

It was ten-thirty. Tinny piano music clattered from the saloon on Hawk's left. On his right, the current opera singers tittered like crazy birds within the McCormick House's clapboard walls. Several surreys were parked before the establishment's wrought iron fence. A man in a top hat stood near the gate, reading the latest edition of the *Yankton Press and Dakotan* while smoking a stogie, the aromatic smoke drifting back to Hawk.

When Hawk had stood hidden in the shadows for nearly an hour, a short man with a slight paunch stepped out of a saloon directly across the street from the opera house. Silhouetted against the long, curved window behind him, he wore a suit, a vest, and a high-peaked, broad-brimmed hat with a Montana crease.

All day, Hawk had been keeping an eye on County Attorney Benton T. Parks, who now stood left of the batwing doors, hands in his pockets, swinging his gaze slowly up and down the street and chewing a cigar stub, nervously biding his time. Finally, he stepped forward, removed a set of reins from a hitch rack, walked around the rack, and grabbed the saddle horn of a tall, piebald stallion with a black mane and tail.

Parks poked his left boot in the stirrup, and had to hop several times on his right foot before he finally hoisted himself into the hurricane deck. Uncertainly, he reined the horse away from the rack, adjusted his hat with a flick of his hand, then booted the horse into a trot, heading east between the oil lamps and boardwalks crowded with Yankton's Friday-night revelers.

Hawk mounted his buckskin and gigged the horse around the opera house. The man in the top hat looked up from his paper and nodded a casual greeting. Hawk swung the buckskin right, swerving around the opera crowd's parked buggies.

Ahead, Parks's silhouette faded into the shadows. Hawk booted the buckskin into a trot, then adjusted his speed, staying only close enough to the county attorney to see the man's bobbing shadow and the occasional, silvery swish of his horse's tail.

Hawk swerved right onto Dakota Avenue. He crossed Marne Creek slowly, so the buckskin's hooves made only a soft tapping on the bridge's wooden boards over the rippling black water, then gigged him into a lurching canter

until once again Parks's shadow bobbed ahead, between
two lines of giant cottonwoods.

It was just as Mr. Thomas had said. Parks seemed to
have some business away from town.

Beyond the cottonwood branches, fleecy clouds obscured the stars. A long ways off, a farmer's dog yam-
mered in frustrated tones, as though at a treed coon or
porcupine.

Ahead, Parks's silhouette dissolved into inky shadows, and Hawk rose up in his saddle, staring intently over
the buckskin's head.

A man's voice lifted amidst the soft screech of
grasshoppers and the breeze in the cottonwoods, and
Hawk jerked back on the buckskin's reins. The horse
turned quarter-wise, and Hawk peered ahead, squinting.
Another man's voice rose, then another's in response, and
then came the soft thuds of horse hooves—at least three
sets—fading into the eastern distance.

Hawk squinted into the darkness, thinking.

Parks had picked up two other riders—bodyguards,
no doubt, ensuring that the attorney wouldn't be separated from his gold. They'd be watching their back trail
very closely now.

Hawk urged his horse ahead slowly, straining his ears
to listen, squinting into the shadowy night, the trees and
brush buffeting along both sides of the trail. After a mile,
another trail intersected with the main one on the right,
climbing along the shoulder of a low, wooded hill, disappearing under a clearing, star-streaked sky.

Leaning out from the buckskin, Hawk saw the three
sets of fresh horse tracks turning off the main trail and
gouging the hard, stone-pocked dirt of the secondary

trail. Two rode single file along the left track. The other man trotted along the right.

Hawk gigged the buckskin forward and stopped when voices rose on the breeze. The sounds were stationary; Parks and the other two men had stopped.

Hawk reined the buckskin off the trail and up the hill, into a dense stand of burr oaks. He dismounted, ground-hitched the buckskin, shucked his rifle from the saddle boot, and ducked through the low branches, weaving around trunks, until he was kneeling behind a stump along the hill's shoulder, facing south.

Below, in the meadow on the other side of the trail, was a cemetery, the tombstones and crosses silhouetted in the vague, milky light of a moon scudding out from behind violet-edged clouds. On one knee, holding his Henry across the other thigh, the lawman stared at the three men milling thirty yards away, near a crooked wooden cross and a mound of sod chunks and freshly turned soil.

"Hurry," Parks ordered, nervous. "I don't have all night." He stood off to the left of the other two men, who were toeing shovels into the grave. He looked around owlishly, then brought a hand to his mouth and tipped his head back, drinking from a small flask.

"You said we was supposed to watch your back," one of the shovelers grumbled. "Didn't say nothin' in the saloon about diggin'." He was the same height as Parks, but wider and broader in the shoulders, with a broad-brimmed, floppy hat. He wore a pistol on each hip.

"Didn't I?"

"Sure as hell didn't," the other man said, his high, raspy voice strained with exertion.

Parks jerked his head around nervously, casting wary glances around the cemetery and the hill where Hawk crouched. Even in the dark, his hat looked ridiculously big for his body. "Don't know why they had to bury it so damn deep. They knew I'd be on edge, that's why. Funny boys. Okay, okay, I'll throw in another twenty-five for each of you. Now, shut up and dig."

The bigger man paused, glanced at the other man, and shook his head. He kicked his shovel into the dirt and tossed a load at the feet of Parks, who leapt back suddenly. "Hey, watch where you're throwin' that stuff. These shoes cost more than both your cow ponies put together."

The men dug for several minutes, grunting.

"If we dig up a body, I'm lightin' a shuck," said the man with the higher voice. "I got no truck with the dead."

"I told you this has nothing to do with dead people."

"Yeah, but you also said—" The bigger man stopped, froze. He probed with the shovel. "Hey, I think I got somethin'."

"Pull it up," Parks said.

The two shovelers got down on their knees, dug with their hands. The big man lifted something. "Jesus, it's heavy!"

The two men fumbled around with an object, brushing dirt away, pulling away what appeared, from Hawk's vantage point, to be a burlap wrap.

"Holy shit, it's an ingot!" exclaimed the man with the raspy voice. "Has to be five thousand dollars worth of gold here!"

"Should be five thousand, two hundred, and fifty," said Parks as he reached into his coat and produced a pistol, the barrel glinting in the moonlight. Hawk heard the hammer click back.

The two shovelers, still on their knees, looked up at the little attorney with the big Stetson and a pocket pistol clenched in his fist.

"Hold on!" the bigger man shouted.

Parks backed up a step, hesitating, glancing around quickly. He'd like to have had his two "bodyguards" accompany him back to town, in case Meade's men bushwhacked him and took back their gold. But if he killed them closer to town, his shots might be heard. "I can't let anyone speak of this . . . ever." Parks's pistol popped, stabbing flames, wafting smoke.

The big man grunted and jerked back. "You double-crossin' son of a bitch!" He reached for the pistol on his left hip, but Parks shot him again, through the head, blowing his hat off, before he could pull the gun from his holster.

The other man hadn't gone for his holstered pistol or the rifles leaning against a nearby tombstone. Shocked, he'd tried gaining his feet, but fell back on the ground, groaning and throwing up his hands, palms out as if to shield himself from bullets. "No! Please! I—!"

Parks's pistol popped, the slug tearing through the shoveler's left hand and exiting, spraying blood, and plunging into his neck. The man gagged and rolled onto a shoulder, clutching his neck with both hands as Parks stepped forward, extended the pistol, and fired another round through the man's head, just above his left ear.

The man thrashed, kicking his legs as if trying to run, turning a near circle on his hip before he kicked once more and lay still.

Parks stared down at the two dead men, breathing heavily. The three horses, ten yards behind him, gave startled nickers and soft whinnies as they tugged at their reins tied to a low shrub.

Parks mopped his forehead with a handkerchief, then returned his pistol to the holster under his coat and picked up the gold bar with both hands. Shoulders drawn forward by the gold's weight, the little man carried the bar to his piebald standing with the other two horses. He placed the ingot inside a satchel looped over his saddle horn, then mounted up, reined the horse onto the trail, and gigged it into a gallop back the way he'd come.

The horse had taken only three strides when a rope dropped over Parks's head and chest, drawing instantly taut and pinning his arms to his sides. He found himself sailing ass-over-teakettle off the animal's rump, losing his hat and hitting the ground on his back, gasping for air.

His head reeling, Parks stared at the star-dusted, moonlit sky. He tried to move his arms, but they were pinned fast. A shadow moved to his left and behind, and then a man was standing over him, peering down—a tall, broad-shouldered man in a frock coat and flat-brimmed black hat.

The man held a stock rope coiled in his right hand. The left hand held the loop taut around Parks's chest.

"What the hell . . . ?" Parks muttered.

"You sold out my boy, Parks," Hawk said.

"Hawk!" Parks stared up at the tall silhouette of Gideon Hawk, the dark eyes shining like obsidian chips in the starlight. Parks gasped and struggled against the rope, but the more he struggled, the tighter it pulled, cutting into his arms. He gave up and lay still.

"Hawk . . . no . . . please . . ."

"Weren't enough witnesses, eh?" Hawk's chuckle was humorless. "The old woman who talked to Ned in Crossroads—she wasn't trustworthy because she wasn't *wearing her glasses*?"

"It's the way of the law, Deputy," Parks croaked, trying to put some steel in his voice.

"Don't call me Deputy, you dung beetle. I don't work for you anymore. I don't work for *any* court anymore. And neither do you."

"Hawk, listen . . ."

Hawk stepped forward, placed his left boot on Parks's chest, and pressed down, pinching off Parks's wind. "O'Malley's testimony couldn't be trusted because the rain might've obscured his *view*? I couldn't be trusted because, being so personally involved in the matter, I was overcome with *emotion*? Isn't that what you wrote in that brief?"

Hawk removed his foot from Parks's chest, crouched down, jerked the rope up around the man's neck, and drew it tight. Raking in a deep breath, his eyes snapping wide with fear, Parks raised his hands to his neck, tried to loosen the noose. Peering up into Hawk's face, he saw a two-day growth of beard below the flinty eyes, the lawman's jaws set hard, lips pursed thin with fury.

The attorney had known the lawman to be a cool, objective professional. That man was gone, replaced by a raging, blood-hungry wolf.

"No . . ." Parks begged, clawing at the rope.

Hawk stood and, holding the rope taut with his right hand, hooked his left beneath Parks's left arm, wrenched the man to his feet. "I've done passed sentence on you, Mr. Prosecutor. Time for your reckoning."

Hawk dug a leather strap from the pocket of his frock coat and used it to tie Parks's hands behind his back, Parks crying out as the hide cut into the skin, cutting off the blood flow.

"Please, Hawk . . . Gideon . . . you don't understand the strain I've been under."

Hawk shoved the man toward his horse standing twenty yards up the trail, reins dangling. "You mean, fucking the dance-hall girl?"

"If it got out, my career . . . my life . . . would be ruined. I didn't want to let Meade out, but I had to."

"What about the gold?" Hawk said, giving the man another brusque shove toward the stallion.

"Christ, after all they put me through . . . having three men show up in my house unannounced . . . the threats to my life, my career . . . Why not take the money? It wasn't going to change the fact that Meade is free."

"Practical man." Hawk shoved Parks again. The attorney stumbled forward and fell to his knees. His breath rattled up from his chest. The sweat streaking his face glistened in the starlight.

"Dear God, you're not really going to do this. . . ."

Drawing air sharply through his nostrils, Hawk pulled the man to his feet, grabbed the horse's reins, and forced the man onto the saddle.

"Take me back to Yankton," Parks pleaded, his voice shaking. "I'll stand before the judge. What I've done is wrong. I admit that."

"Noble of you." Hawk led the horse back along the trail, toward the cottonwood standing on the right side of the trail, up the hill about fifteen yards, its branches splayed against the stars and rising moon. A cool breeze rattled the leaves and made a branch creak like an unoiled hinge.

"This isn't your job, Gideon," Parks said softly, the strain in his voice betraying his terror. He swallowed. "You can't judge me . . . only arrest me."

Hawk said nothing.

"Hawk, please!" the prosecutor barked, exploding. "You're not a vigilante. You're the most upstanding lawman I've ever known. Take me back to Yankton, throw me in jail, but for Christ's sake, don't do this. Think of your own career."

Hawk positioned the horse beneath a branch arching twenty feet above the hillside. He stepped away from the horse, looked up into the tree, judging the exact distance to the branch. He gave a couple practice swings with the rope coil, then let it loose. The coil flew over the branch and hit the ground with a thump and rustle.

"Meade hung my boy, Jubal," Hawk said. "My wife, Linda, hung herself the very next day out of grief." He stooped to retrieve the rope coil, then straightened and regarded Parks, wide eyes spitting fire. "I arrested that son of a bitch, trusted you to prosecute him."

Hawk laughed, shaking his head and showing his teeth. "And you set him free, killed those two down there, and took the money."

Parks stared back at the lawman, the prosecutor's chest rising and falling sharply.

"Tell me, Mr. Prosecutor," Hawk said tightly, tying the rope around the tree's broad trunk. "Did you give one thought to my son and my wife?"

"Of course I did, Gideon."

When he'd tied the knot, Hawk stepped up to within ten feet of Parks. "Should have given 'em two." He drew his revolver, aimed the barrel skyward, and thumbed back the hammer.

"You bastard," Parks said. "This is no way for a man like me to die."

Hawk smiled.

"You may be killing me. But you're killing yourself here, too. You'll be haunted by this every day for the rest of your life. Sure as I'm gonna die, you are, too . . . just slower."

Hawk pulled the trigger. The horse bolted out from beneath Parks's hanging body, bounding off along the slope with an angry whinny. Parks choked and kicked furiously, as if at some unseen object in the air before him. His cheeks turned crimson and his eyes bulged as he twisted left, then right, six feet above the ground.

The prosecutor's macabre death dance, accompanied by sighs, gasps, and chokes, continued for several minutes, winding slowly down until Parks gave one last, half-hearted kick, and the smell of shit and urine emanated from his broadcloth slacks.

Blood surging in his temples, Hawk stared up at the dead attorney, whose neck had been stretched a good six inches, his tongue swollen and protruding from one corner of his mouth, like a tired dog's.

13.

NEVER AGAIN

HAWK spat and holstered his pistol. He gave the lawyer's body one last glance as it turned slightly on the creaking rope, then turned and started up the hill toward his horse.

Behind him, a rifle shot pierced the quiet, the bullet whistling over Hawk's right shoulder and tearing through Parks's left leg before plunking into the cottonwood.

Ramming a fresh round into the Henry's breech, Hawk dove behind the tree as two more shots chewed up the sod around him, a third crunching into the cottonwood's bole, spraying bark. He rose to his knees and edged a look around the trunk. A rifle flashed in the graveyard, about fifty yards away and slightly left, the slug plowing into a low branch with a screeching ricochet.

Another shot—from the right and about the same distance away—blew the heel off Parks's left shoe, giving the limp body a spin before grinding bark inches from Hawk's face.

Hawk turned his back to the tree, facing uphill and holding the rifle straight up and down, making his body narrow, so the cottonwood shielded him completely.

He looked to his left and right, hearing nothing, seeing no sign of the shooters trying to flank him.

"Come on out here, amigo," a voice sounded from the cemetery. "We wanna have a little talk . . . 'bout the gold."

Hawk smiled. He pushed himself forward, dropped onto his knees, and crawled straight out from the tree. Crabbing up the hill, he kept his head down, his rifle down low in the grass, where the moonlight and starlight couldn't reflect off its chasing.

Another flat, cracking shot split the night's breeze-whispering silence, the slug drilling the tree with a solid plunk.

Hawk wove around two oaks and a spindly ironwood, ducked through gooseberry scrub smelling like overripe fruit and skunk, and crawled over the hill's crest. When he'd crawled another ten feet down the other side, he stood and ran to his right, heading east toward the cemetery trail's intersection with the main road.

He ran south across the trail, through a shallow gully, and along the cemetery's eastern edge until he'd reached the trees behind it.

Intending to flank the shooters, he moved west and stopped at the edge of the trees and shrubs, staring into the cemetery. While he'd been moving, the gunmen had been moving, too, shouting at the cottonwood tree on the hillside, shouting at each other, and triggering occasional shots up the hill.

As far as Hawk could tell, one man remained in the

cemetery, while the other two were moving forward. They were either at the north edge of the cemetery or were climbing the hill toward the tree. The one below was covering them, loosing steady shots, the slugs pounding the tree with heavy, cracking whumps. Another man triggered two quick shots as well, the flashes marking his position about twenty yards down from the tree and right.

Hawk ran crouching forward and quartering west. When he'd run halfway through the cemetery, he stopped and raised his Henry. A man stood fifteen feet away, his back to Hawk, crouching over his lowered rifle as he thumbed shells from his cartridge belt into the breech.

He was about Hawks's height, wearing a duster and a crisp, brown derby. He stiffened, sensing Hawk behind him. Turning quickly, he raised his rifle, shock and terror etched on his flat face with its neatly trimmed beard and mustache.

Before he could level the rifle, Hawk drilled him through the right cheek. He fell back against the gravestone, as if taking a hurried seat, and collapsed on his left shoulder, rifle dropping between his spread legs. The derby fell off, as if an afterthought.

Three more shots rose from the hillside as Hawk set his rifle in the grass. He picked up the dead man's rifle, straightened, and jacked a shell into the Winchester's breech.

"He ain't behind the tree," one of the men on the hill yelled to another.

Hawk aimed the rifle up the hill and popped off a shot.

"Goddamnit, White, he ain't behind the tree. Stop shootin'!"

Hawk raised the rifle above his head and waved it, grinning to himself and staring up the hill, where Parks's body hung slack from the cottonwood branch, chin tipped to his chest. On either side of the big tree, two shadowy figures moved up to the hill's crest, guns held before them, weaving through the widely scattered oaks, and disappeared down the other side.

Hawk tossed the dead man's rifle down and picked up his own. He replaced the spent shell in the breech, then sat on a gravestone, crossing his ankles and resting his rifle over his right shoulder. He leaned down, plucked a weed, and chewed it.

He sat there for a good fifteen minutes before something moved on the hill. Voices carried down the slope— piss-burned voices, garbled at first by the breeze and crickets.

Then: ". . . woulda got out here sooner, we woulda had that gold. Now, what in God's name are we gonna tell Mr. Priest?"

"Who was that bastard, anyway?"

The first man cursed. "Some asshole who got wind of the plan, and followed Parks out from town to steal the gold." He cursed again. "If we coulda caught his horse, somethin' in the saddlebags might've identified him."

They were halfway down the hill, tramping through the grass, the man on Hawk's left carrying his rifle in both hands across his chest. The other held his own carbine straight down along his right leg. Both wore dark brown dusters and derbies, their trousers tucked into their high-topped boots.

The man on the right tripped and stumbled, nearly dropping to one knee. When he got both feet beneath him again, he said, "We'll wait for the son of a bitch in town, show him what he got himself into."

When the two men were nearly to the hill's base, the one on the left peered toward Hawk still lounging against the grave marker. "Any sign of him down here, Whitey?"

Hawk squeezed the rifle stock but kept the barrel on his shoulder. "Nope."

"We saw his horse but couldn't catch it," said the man on the right. "Our friend must've cut out on foo—" He stopped suddenly, one boot on the trail, fifteen feet away from Hawk. He stared intensely at Hawk, whose face was hidden by the low-canted brim of his hat.

The second man slowed and looked at the first man, puzzled. "What's wrong with you, Rip?" He followed the first man's gaze to Hawk and, halfway across the trail, stopped, jerking forward at the waist from the force of his own momentum, nearly dropping his rifle.

"That ain't Whitey," Rip said.

The other man didn't say anything. He stared at Hawk. Gideon could hear the men breathing, imagined he could hear their hearts thudding behind their ribs. Scared shitless for their own wormy hides, but would kill a man for a bar of gold. These men who worked for Meade were little better than Meade himself.

Almost casually, Hawk slid his rifle off his shoulder, lowered the barrel into the palm of his right hand, and shot both men where they stood.

He stepped forward through the lingering gun smoke, stooped down, and pressed a finger to the first man's neck.

Dead.

He moved to the right, where the other man, Rip, was

crawling along the trail, heading east at a snail's pace. He'd lost his hat and his rifle, and his long, gray-brown hair swirled about his head. He kept bringing his knees down on his duster, tearing the shoulder seams. He grunted and panted miserably, terrified.

Hawk bent down and thrust the barrel into a gaping blood splotch low on the left side of Rip's back, where the bullet had exited after punching through his belly. The man cried out and collapsed.

Hawk said, "You tell me where to find the man who hired you, or I'm gonna rebore this hole from the other side and leave you to die slow."

"Oh, Jesus!"

"Where is he?"

"Please—!"

Hawk shoved the rifle deeper into the man's back. "You got one more chance."

"Oh, Christ." Rip sucked air through gritted teeth. *"Bonnie Springs, Arizona!"*

Hawk raised the barrel to the back of Rip's head and pulled the trigger.

"Obliged," he said, and walked away.

When Hawk had found his own buckskin, he ran down Parks's piebald stallion, dug the gold bar out of the dead attorney's satchel, and placed it in his own saddlebags. Climbing back into the hurricane deck, he booted the buckskin due south.

He traveled all night, stopping twice at farmsteads only to rest and water his horse at stock tanks, then riding on, bringing Crossroads up out of the rolling prairie an hour after dawn.

He rode around the east edge of the little town and napped in the cemetery, near the graves of his wife and son, while the unsaddled buckskin grazed on a long picket rope near the creek.

When he woke, the sun was high, tilting shadows out from the shrubs and cottonwoods outlying the cemetery. He stood before the graves for a long time, his hat in his hands, the washed-out, late-summer leaves churning over his head. His beloved son and wife lay before him, under two twin mounds of dirt over which thin, pale-green grasses were beginning to grow. A cruel joke played on him by the Fates.

Why?

Hadn't he always tried to live morally and to set a good example for others?

Hadn't he always been a just and fair lawman, putting evil men away so that others could live without fear?

Why did Jubal and Linda have to die? They were innocent.

More from habit than anything else, Hawk tried to think of a prayer to say, but none found its way to his lips. Still, he bowed his head. Tears ran down his cheeks. His shoulders jerked and shuddered. His sadness enveloped him like a second skin, impossible to shrug off or see beyond.

He would never again fish with his son, or walk along the creek-side trail on a golden, breezy afternoon like this, carrying a stringer of glistening perch for Linda to fry for supper.

No more family Thanksgivings. No more Christmases. No more outings to cut firewood. No more quiet evenings around the fire—just him, Linda, and Jubal.

Finally, he dropped to one knee, ran his right sleeve across his face, and sniffed. He said simply, "I love you. You'll be avenged."

Hawk's chest convulsed. He sobbed.

He'd never see Jubal grown—and what a fine man he would have made, too.

Hawk squeezed his eyes closed and threw his head back on his shoulders. *"Why?"* The single word echoed like a thunderclap.

He stood, donned his hat, again sleeved tears from his cheeks, and walked down the hill to the creek. He tacked up the buckskin, and followed the shortest route to his house, dreading walking inside and confronting the ghosts and demons that haunted the place now.

He opened the kitchen door and walked in, stepping softly. He ran his eyes over the kitchen cabinets, over the iron skillets and tin pots still hanging where Linda had last hung them. He stopped in the short hall and peered into the living room, at the few humble chairs, tables, and wall hangings he and Linda had gathered over the years.

On the table beside the rocker in which Gideon had read to Jubal every night he was home and not off chasing outlaws, were a half-dozen horses the boy had carved. Each had its own distinctive posture. Some galloped, manes buffeting. Some rose up on hind legs as if clawing at the sky. The big purple-black one crow-hopped, its eyes wide and body twisting, as though it had a lariat loop around its neck.

"No one's ever gonna break that one, Pa," the boy had said once, a romantic light in his eyes.

Hawk went into his and Linda's bedroom, found a war bag in the closet, and packed it with a single change of

clothes, a tintype of himself, Linda, and Jubal, a big
bowie knife with a hide-wrapped handle and tooled-
leather sheath.

As an afterthought, he added to his war bag one of
Jubal's horses—the black stallion rising tall on its back
legs, as if raging at the heavens.

When he'd set the war bag on the porch, he came back
inside, found a scrap of paper, scribbled a few words on
it, then crossed the living room to the front door. He took
a last look around.

Choking down the hard, dry knot in his throat, he
turned, stepped onto the porch, and closed the door behind him.

Never again . . .

He hung the note on a nail for his next-door neighbor,
the Widow Ellingson. It read in large, scrawled letters,
THE HOUSE AND EVERYTHING IN IT ARE YOURS
TO DO WITH AS YOU WANT. WON'T BE BACK.
GIDEON HAWK.

Clutching the war bag, he walked around to the back,
where he'd tied his horse to Linda's clothesline. He hung
two canteens and the war bag over his saddle horn,
mounted up, and looked once more at the house, running
his eyes over the windows and doors, over the clapboards
that were due a fresh coat of paint. Hawk had planned for
him and Jubal to paint the house next spring.

Ignoring the tears veiling his vision, he booted the
buckskin out of the yard and down the dusty lane.

He rode to the livery barn and traded the buckskin for
a big paint and a stocky claybank with good staying
power.

"Marshal Hawk, if I didn't know better, I'd say you

were plannin' on bein' gone for quite some time," the liveryman, Ralph Anderson, said.

The corners of Anderson's gray-blue eyes spoked with befuddlement as he regarded the unshaven lawman. The marshal's normally warm and animated eyes were now deep-sunk, flat, and brooding, his usually well-brushed clothes now dusty and worn, torn buttons dangling.

Hawk climbed onto the paint and took the claybank's lead line in his right fist.

"Yah, that's what I'd say," the liveryman repeated, obviously prodding Hawk for details.

"Good day, Anderson."

Hawk booted the paint into a trot, jerking the claybank along behind, weaving around freight and farm wagons and ignoring the hails of men he'd known for many years, keeping his eyes ahead, his back straight.

Behind him, the townsmen frowned after him, puzzled.

Hawk followed the stage road west. A few minutes after he'd left Crossroads, Mr. Thomas's Place rose from the sandy, western buttes before him—a tall, leaning, weather-beaten shack glowing dully in the late-afternoon sun, sooty pine smoke wafting from the stone chimney abutting the shack's east side.

Hawk had intended to ride past without stopping, but then a familiar, squeaky voice sounded from the house on the butte to his right.

"Well, I'll be goddamned—there he is *now*!"

Mr. Thomas laughed.

Hawk stopped the paint and turned to the house.

The dwarf stood on the front porch, peering toward Hawk through the railing, both hands gripping the rail on either side and above his man-sized head, his goat's beard ruffling in the breeze. His little-boy jeans were stuffed into the tops of his little black boots.

Another man, full-sized, stood left of Mr. Thomas. He wore a dusty suit, vest, black frock, and a black Plainsman like Hawk's. The hair beneath the hat, curling over the man's collar, was carrot-red.

At the hitch rack before the porch, a dusty, sweat-silvery dun stood, swishing its tail at flies.

Morgan. Shit. When Parks's body was found, the young deputy must've lit out after Hawk.

Hawk turned and gigged the paint forward along the trail.

Luke Morgan's voice rose behind him. "Marshal Hawk!"

Hawk kept riding. Like a warlock's cry, Mr. Thomas's raspy cackle traveled down the butte from the shack. Shortly, hooves pounded the trail behind Hawk, and saddle leather creaked.

"Gideon!" Morgan called. "Hold up, Hawk!"

Hawk cantered steadily forward, the second horse trailing four feet off the paint's left rear hip. Morgan rode up on Hawk's right, edging his dun ahead, then reaching over and grabbing the paint's bridle bit, halting Hawk's horse as well as his own.

"Gideon, goddamnit, did you—?" Morgan stopped when he saw the Henry carbine aimed at his belly. Hawk stared at him coldly. But it was only a blurred tintype of the man whom Morgan had known. Hawk's skin was sallow, the eyes bitter and grief-stricken. His clothes hung on his gaunt frame, as if he hadn't slept or eaten in weeks.

"You lynched Parks," Morgan said, realizing the truth.

"Yes."

Morgan stared at him uncomprehendingly, his eyes dropping to the badge pinned to Hawk's vest. "You're a *lawman*!"

"I upheld the law. Parks is dead."

"You're not a judge."

"I am now."

Morgan studied Hawk with scorn, narrowed eyes probing. "Gideon, look at yourself. I know you're grieving, but you're not in your right mind."

"Step down from the saddle, Deputy."

Morgan looked confused. "What?"

"Step down. I'm takin' your horse."

Morgan shook his head slowly. "I have to take you back to Yankton."

"You're not taking me anywhere, Luke. No one stands between me and Meade."

The red-haired deputy glanced at the rifle, narrowed his right eye. "You'd kill me, Gid?"

"If you forced my hand, Luke, I would."

Morgan's pale, freckled cheeks flushed crimson. "You taught me to follow the law. Remember, 'No Judge Lynch,' Gideon?"

Regret raked at Hawk's mind. He'd taught Morgan nearly everything the young deputy knew about law enforcement, and had shared his own ideals with the boy. Now Hawk was turning on him.

Their friendship was something else for Hawk to bury, something else to mourn.

"I was wrong," Hawk said. "Didn't realize that in some cases the law don't work."

"Parks didn't work. One man didn't do his job. That doesn't mean the whole system is corrupt."

Hawk's eyes narrowed. "Everybody's corrupt. Step down, Deputy. I'm takin' your horse so you can't follow me."

"Don't do this, Gid." Morgan's voice cracked with emotion. "You'll be hunted like the men you hunted."

Hawk laughed without mirth. "As I recall, you've wanted to do the same thing."

Softly, with deep sadness, Morgan said, "But I always had you there to stop me, to turn me back right. . . ."

"Step down," Hawk said.

"The lawmen need to be as vile as the law-breakers— that it?"

"Sounds about right." Hawk thumbed his rifle hammer back and canted the barrel toward Morgan's chest.

Morgan looked at the rifle, then at Hawk gazing coldly into the younger man's eyes. A tear inching down his cheek, Morgan swung his right leg over the horse's rump and stepped down to the ground.

His voice was sad and bewildered. "You're one of them now, Gideon."

Hawk reached over and grabbed the dun's reins. "Just takin' the law to their level." He booted the paint forward. "I'll leave your horse up the trail a few miles."

He stared at Morgan hard across his shoulder. "Don't follow me, Luke. I'll kill you."

He disappeared around the shoulder of a hill and was gone.

14.

SALOON DE PARIS

H AWK sold his horses in Denver, then hopped the
train to Prescott, Arizona Territory, where he bought
a couple more mounts as well as trail supplies.

Two days later, midafternoon, he rode down off a bald
ridge into a rocky valley in which a few gaunt cabins and
board shacks lined a shallow creek. Most of the shacks
were empty, weeds grown up around their foundations,
open doors and empty windows staring unseeingly, like
the eye sockets of rotting skulls.

Only a saloon at the far end of the ghost town showed
signs of life—smoke curling from a chimney pipe in the
corrugated tin roof, three dusty horses standing before the
hitch rack in the wheel-spoke position, heads together,
butts spaced wide. The front porch was shored up with
rocks that had tumbled down from the looming ridges,
rotten floorboards replaced with unpainted pine planks.

Hawk gave the place only a passing glance as he followed the trail across the chuckling stream, through a gap

in the southern rock wall, and down an easy slope through pines and aspens, the aspen leaves bright, fall-mountain yellow. Pine smoke from the saloon's chimney pipe tanged the air, and hovered as a sunlit blue fog against the trees.

When the trail forked a half mile from the ghost town, Hawk stopped his steeldust gelding and the sorrel following on a lead line. He stared down each fork, the left disappearing into the aspen forest, the right curving over a rocky hill shoulder. By the look of the weeds and rocks and fallen branches, neither had been used much in the past months or even years.

A post with several weather-scarred wooden arrows stood at the tip of the V of the two forking trails. Several arrows bearing the names of mining settlements pointed to each trail. None of the arrows named the town Hawk was looking for, but a gap between the planks indicated that one was missing.

He reined the steeldust around and headed back the way he had come, splitting the mountain gap, splashing across the stream, and pulling up before the saloon. A sign hanging over the porch was too faded to read until he stood under it: THE SALOON DE PARIS.

Hawk tied the horses to the hitch rack, mounted the creaky porch, and stepped through the door, two sets of rusty hinges on both sides of the frame all that remained of the batwings. There wasn't much inside, either—just a few tables scattered right of several six-foot planks laid across beer kegs. Except for the buzz of several flies bouncing against the dirt-streaked front window, the place was silent.

When Hawk's eyes adjusted to the gloom, he saw a

big, curly-headed man sitting on a stool behind the bar, trimming his nails with a folding barlow knife. Three men sat at a table against the opposite wall, one more at a table farther back in the gloom, half-reclining in his chair, both feet crossed on the chair across the table.

Hawk returned his gaze to the big man behind the bar, his face all freckled and tallow, with shaggy brows under the mussed mop of brown curls. The man reluctantly lifted his gaze from the nail he was deftly slicing, looked at Hawk dully.

"Whiskey," Hawk said.

The man climbed off his stool, set the knife on the bar, and grabbed a bottle and a shot glass from the bowed shelf behind him. Doing so, he startled a mouse that had been sitting there, eating something. The mouse squeaked angrily, ran to the end of the shelf and down the wall. The bartender filled the glass and slid it toward Gideon.

"Fifty cents," the man said in a voice so deep and raspy as to be nearly inaudible. If you taught English to the progeny of a bear crossed with a pig, it would sound like the bartender.

"Steep," Hawk said.

"You know where you are?"

"A fair piece from the beaten path."

"Give the man a cigar."

Hawk tossed the coins on the bar and tossed back the shot. As the bartender gathered the coins in his pudgy hands, Hawk asked, "Which trail fork leads to Bonnie Springs?"

The big man froze, blinking, and Hawk began to wonder if he'd heard him. A flush rose up from the man's three chins.

"Who's goin' to Bonnie Springs?" a voice said behind Hawk.

Slowly, Gideon turned.

The three men at the table against the far wall stared at him. Two wore deputy sheriff's stars pinned to their shabby wool shirts. The third, a small gent with Mexican-dark skin and a thick mustache curling over both corners of his mouth, sat between the deputies, his arms drawn taut behind his chair. He wasn't wearing a hat. His right eye was swollen nearly closed, and both puffy lips were crusted with dried blood.

Gideon wasn't sure which of the two deputies had spoken. He ran his gaze between both. It had been nearly two weeks since he'd hanged Parks. News of a rogue lawman had no doubt been sizzling through the telegraph way stations throughout the frontier.

"I am," he said.

"Got business in Bonnie Springs, do ye?" asked the man on the right. He was thirty or so, unshaven, with dull eyes beneath the broad, frayed brim of his sombrero.

"I do."

The two deputies shared glances, the one on the left smirking slightly. He looked at Hawk, running his eyes up and down the tall, dark-clad man at the bar.

The deputy's gray-blue eyes fairly glowed in a shaft of light angling through the window. His right hand was wrapped around his shot glass. The other hand was beneath the table. "Well, Bonnie Springs don't have no business with you, *Marshal*. Ride wide."

Hawk dropped his chin, lowered his eyes to his chest. His badge was pinned to his vest, just visible under the frock's left lapel. He'd intended to remove it, but every time he'd begun doing so, something had made him stop. Even after what he'd done to Parks, wearing the badge felt right.

Resting his elbows on the bar top, Hawk looked from one deputy to the other. His eyes were flat. Both men stared back at him, backs taut, eyes partially hidden by the brims of their hats.

The man between them flushed fearfully and fidgeted around in his chair, hands apparently handcuffed behind the chair back. He rolled his eyes to the men on either side of him, then Hawk. Sweat beaded his forehead.

"Please," he said softly, squirming and making his chair creak. "Do not shoot, *por favor. . . .*"

Hawk looked from the Mexican prisoner to the deputy on his left, then to the one on his right. They had sluggish, heavy-handed looks about them. He could probably take them both, but there was no point in drawing attention to himself.

He conjured a smile, his untrimmed mustache lifting, unshaven cheeks spreading. He raised his hands, palm out. "I reckon I can take a hint."

"That's good," growled the man on the right. "It's always good when a man can take a hint. I've always said that. Saves so much . . . time."

Staring at Hawk, he spread his lips, showing a silver tooth coated in chewing tobacco as he grinned. He threw back his drink, added the empty glass to the several other empties on the table, then shoved back his chair and stood. Still smiling at Hawk, he fished a key from his shirt pocket, and crouched behind the Mexican. When he'd unlocked the handcuffs, he straightened, stuffed the handcuffs behind his cartridge belt, jerked the Mexican to his feet, and shoved him toward the door.

He raised his hat to Hawk. "Nice chattin'."

"I enjoyed it."

The deputy followed his prisoner outside. His boots thudded on the squeaky porch steps.

Hawk looked at the other deputy, who sat in his chair for a few seconds, then rose slowly. His left hand on his pistol butt, he moved to the door, stopped, and turned toward Hawk. He backed through the open door, then turned and descended the porch steps to the street.

Outside, saddle leather creaked. Hooves thudded on the hard street, and after a few seconds, silence. Only the flies buzzing against the windows and around the deputies' empty shot glasses.

Hawk pushed off the bar and took a step toward the door.

"I'd give 'em a few minutes." It was the man sitting in the shadows at the other end of the room.

Hawk stopped and turned toward him, one eyebrow cocked. Because of the gloom, he couldn't see much more than a silhouette.

"They may not look like much," the man said, "but they're both handy with their six-shooters, and they'll be watchin' their back trail."

Hawk stared into the shadows, then turned and planted both elbows on the bar.

"Reckon I'll have another shot," he told the barman, who stood regarding him tensely, thin lips sucked into the folds of his lumpy face.

Hawk nursed the drink for several minutes, hearing the flies sputter against the window and the low, steady roar of the stream outside the saloon. He threw the last of his whiskey back, winced at the burn as he set the glass on the counter, and tossed down some change. He ran the back of his hand across his mustache, then headed for the door.

"The right fork'll take you to Bonnie Springs, Mr. Hawk," said the man in the shadows.

Hawk turned around. The man still lounged back in his chair, ankles crossed on the chair opposite. He lifted his hand to his mouth, throwing back a drink. Hawk squinted, but he couldn't make out the man's features.

"Obliged," Hawk said, then turned through the door and descended the steps to the street.

Hawk followed the trail's right fork for two hours, until darkness settled, thick as a velvet shroud trimmed with glittering jewels, over the high mountain plateau. He made camp in a hollow thirty yards off the trail, tying his horses to picket pins in high grama grass, then climbed a knoll.

Down the long, sloping grade, about a mile away, a pinprick of orange light flickered in the darkness—most likely the deputies' cook fire, barely visible through the inky-black mass of woods.

Hawk built his own fire against a rock scarp, surrounded by boulders, cedars, and pines to shield the firelight. A spring-fed rivulet trickled down a nearby ledge. He was arranging his blanket roll, getting ready to turn in, when the soft thuds of hoof falls rose from the darkness and a saddle creaked.

Hawk grabbed his rifle and, ramming a fresh shell into the chamber, crouched behind a boulder.

"Hello the fire. Don't shoot. I'm peaceable." The voice was a hollow sound in the dense night, at once crisp and distant, like a call from the bottom of a well. It owned a familiar, faintly ironic pitch.

"Ride in slow," Hawk ordered. "Keep both hands where I can see 'em."

In the darkness, a man chuckled softly, as if to himself. The hoof thuds rose until horse and rider materialized from the shadows, appearing in the soft firelight between two pine trees. Ten feet from the fire, the man halted the paint, his hands raised to his shoulders. The horse lowered its head and blew.

In the darkness, Hawk could make out little of the man but a ragged, funnel-brimmed cream hat and a long, brown duster with a torn pocket. Only his unshaven jaws were visible beneath the tonguelike oval of shade beneath the lowered hat brim.

The man wasn't dressed like either of the two deputies Hawk had seen in the saloon earlier. Just the same, Hawk looked sharply to his own left and right, then stole a gaze behind, in case a trap had been set and another shooter was trying to draw a bead on him.

"That coffee sure smells good," the rider said. "Mind if I join you?"

Suddenly it occurred to Hawk that the voice belonged to the man from the saloon shadows. He took another look around, then, returning his gaze to the man sitting his horse on the other side of the fire, stepped out from behind the boulder and approached the man slowly. "Step down easy. Any quick movements, you won't see daylight."

"Easy, Hawk. Pull your horns in." Grabbing the horn

with his left hand, the man dismounted and turned to
Hawk. "I'm friend, not foe."

"How do you know me?"

The man stepped forward, until the firelight slid the
shadows up beneath his hat, fully revealing his face.
Squeezing the rifle in both hands, keeping it aimed at the
newcomer's midsection, Hawk studied the man, an inch
or so shorter than Hawk, with a slight paunch swelling
his duster. He did look faintly familiar, but Hawk could
remember neither his name nor where he'd seen him before.

"Joe DeRosso," the man said. "*Sheriff* Joe DeRosso.
We rode together after cattle rustlers up around Horse
Leg Gulch three, four years ago."

Hawk nodded, remembering. DeRosso had been sheriff in the little town of Two-Bit in the Dakota Badlands.
He was also an all-day imbiber, a red-eyed, word-slurring
drunk after four in the afternoon. "What're you doing
down here?"

"Mind if I stake my horse with yours, grab a cup of
that coffee?"

When Gideon nodded again and lowered his Henry,
DeRosso led his horse away from the fire, toward where
Hawk had picketed his two mounts in the tall grass near
the spring. A few minutes later, DeRosso reemerged from
the shadows, his rifle in his left hand, his saddlebags
hanging over his right shoulder.

The man had unbuttoned his duster, and the garment
hung open now, revealing a collarless shirt, a grimy red
undershirt peeking out at the neck, cracked leather suspenders, and patched denims with frayed cuffs hanging
low over his scuffed, high-heeled boots. He wore his pis-

tol butt-forward and high on his right hip, the walnut
grips angled toward his waist.

He tossed his saddlebags down, set his Winchester
against them, then opened the right flap and produced a
dented coffee cup and a whiskey bottle, which he extended to Hawk, who waved it off. DeRosso knelt across
the fire from Hawk and filled his cup from the chugging,
steaming pot, then splashed in some whiskey—all with
his left hand. His right hand was gone, cut off at the wrist,
leaving a grisly stump tucked inside his duster sleeve.

DeRosso sat on a rock, sipped the coffee, then narrowed his eyes over the steaming rim of his cup. "Ran
outta luck in Two-Bit a few years ago, so me and my wife
headed south. I picked up the sheriff's job in Bonnie
Springs." He blew ripples on his coffee and sipped, his
eyes drifting to the fire gaining an angry cast. "An outlaw
turned the citizens against me, and run me out. Took my
job, my *wife,* and my *hand.*" He raised the stump, bitterly
bunching his lips. "An outlaw named Dayton Priest. Hear
of him, Marshal?"

Hawk stared at DeRosso, his face expressionless, skin
drawn tight across his cheekbones.

DeRosso said, "Well, I *know* you heard of his cousin,
Three Fingers Ned Meade. Hell, *that* story's traveled
back and forth across the frontier a half-dozen times!" He
blew on his coffee and sipped.

"Meade was through here a couple weeks ago,"
DeRosso continued. "Had him an entourage from Bonnie
Springs. Priest's men were haulin' his ass south in an old
stagecoach decked out like a royal sleeping chamber."

"How do you know this?"

"I caught a glimpse of Meade when they stopped at the

Paris Saloon. He was lounging on big feather pillows, that broken leg propped high—drunk as a lord and shoutin' orders like a king."

DeRosso chuckled as he splashed more whiskey into his cup. An angry burn rippled through Gideon as he saw it all in his mind's eye—Meade pampering himself like some rich Eastern muckety-muck while Gideon's family rotted in their rotting coffins. Hands shaking slightly, he raised his cup to his lips, sipped his coffee, and swallowed.

He kept the emotion out of his voice. "Meade still in Bonnie Springs?"

DeRosso nodded.

"Where's he stayin'?"

"With his cousin, the sheriff, and the sheriff's lovely wife, the former Ivy DeRosso." The man's voice had lowered a notch, and tightened.

Hawk didn't care about the sheriff's troubled past. He cared only about finding the two men he intended to kill. "Where's Priest live?"

"I'll show you when we ride into Bonnie Springs tomorrow."

Hawk looked at him sharply. "You won't *show* me anything. You'll *tell* me *tonight*."

DeRosso smiled flintily. "Pardon the pun, but I got a bone to pick with Priest." He held up his stump. His eyes were glassy from the whiskey. "I've been waiting in Paris these past eight months, healing and steeling my courage to face Priest one-handed. When I saw Meade in that stage, I decided to wait. I knew you'd be along shortly. We'll face Priest and Meade together—just like we faced them stock thieves."

"No, we won't," Hawk said. "You can scour that from your fool head right now. What you *can* do is tell me where Priest lives. I can probably find Priest himself at the jailhouse, but I want Meade, too, and I take it he's still recovering from that broken leg."

DeRosso's gaze hardened, gained a sulky edge. "He took my wife . . . my *hand*."

"I don't care," Hawk said. "I'm killing those two sons-o'bitches in my own sweet time, in my own sweet way. Don't need some lush of a has-been lawman—a one-handed lawman at that—getting in my way." Hawk shook his head.

DeRosso didn't say anything. He just stared across the fire at Hawk, coffee cup in his hand, the fire's flames leaping in his dark eyes. It was obvious that Hawk had bit the man bone-deep, and deep in Hawk's cold heart, he regretted the harsh words.

Hawk exhaled a long breath. "What happened to you and your wife in Bonnie Springs?"

DeRosso didn't say anything for nearly a minute. He spat to one side. "You got no reason to give a devil's damn about my problems. I lost a town and a wife mainly because, like you said, I'm a lush. You lost a wife and a son through no fault of your own." He finished off his coffee, set down the cup, then picked up the bottle, uncorked it, and took a long pull, his Adam's apple bobbing as he drank.

"Priest's house is a sprawling hacienda along Bonnie Creek, at the south end of town. You can't miss it. Watch your back. Priest's got more 'deputies' than the devil has pitchforks."

He set the bottle on the ground and shoved the cork

into its neck. Standing, he said, "I'll get my horse and head back to the saloon where I belong."

He tucked the bottle back in his saddlebags, slung the bags over his shoulder, and picked up his rifle. He slouched off into the darkness beyond the fire.

Hawk lay down on his bedroll, rested his head against his saddle, and tipped his hat over his eyes, hating himself and feeling sorry for DeRosso. But there was a hardness in him now he could not suppress, even if he wanted to.

The sound of feet crunching gravel and pine needles rose to his ears. Sure that it was only DeRosso returning to plead his case, he was slow to shove his hat back on his head and open his eyes.

When he did, it was too late. A big, broad-shouldered man approached quickly, a double-barreled shotgun aimed at Gideon's head.

One of the two deputies from the saloon chuckled and thumbed back the Greener's hammer with a hollow click. "You're a dead man, Hawk. Dead, dead, *dead*!"

Hawk had just run his eyes up the shotgun's twin bores, to the face of the deputy staring down at him from the other end, when the man's head exploded.

Hawk canted his own head hard left, swinging his right arm up under the shotgun's barrel. The Greener roared, both barrels flashing as the deputy, falling, tripped the triggers.

Hawk clawed his Colt from its holster and, extending the gun toward the second deputy standing several feet behind the other, thumbed the hammer back. But before he could fire the Colt, a rifle cracked in the dark trees to his right. The second deputy stumbled back, grunting and swinging his pistol around, taking a second slug through his breastbone. He fell straight back, bounced off a boulder, and slumped sideways, unmoving.

Ears ringing from the shotgun blast, Hawk looked around, keeping his Colt extended. Smoke wafted in the darkness beyond the umber coals of his fire. Boots crunched gravel and pine needles. A silhouetted figure stepped out of the darkness, holding a rifle over his left shoulder.

The soft light flickered over the face of Joe DeRosso, who shook his head as he gazed down at the two dead deputies. "You're lucky I got good ears."

15.

HACIENDA

O N the brush-roofed ramada of the ancient, crumbling hacienda, Ned Meade flexed his toes, which protruded from the cast on his broken left leg, which he had propped on the railing beside him. He stared down his long, pale nose at the cards fanned out in his hands. Around the table sat three of his cousin's "deputies," smoking cigarettes or cigars and contemplating their own recently dealt pasteboards.

Around the sprawling hacienda, the night's darkness was relieved by the light of a climbing, milky moon. The Sonoran boulders and chaparral stood out in stark relief against the sky. A whore's husky laughter drifted down from a second-story room, its shutters open to the cool desert breeze rife with the smell of piñón and sage.

"How many, Meade?" asked the dealer, a long-boned, bearded man in his early thirties and wearing a black slouch hat, trimmed with hammered silver disks, at a rakish angle.

Meade glanced across the table at the man, gave him a horse-nose sneer. "It's *Mister* Meade to you, sonny."

The man regarded him cautiously under the lowered brim of his hat.

Meade closed his hand, then fanned it open again, like the experienced riverboat cardsharp he once had been. "Just one."

The man to Meade's left chuckled. "Drawing to a straight or a full house, Mr. Meade? Give me three, Rance."

"Got a pair, I see," said the dealer. "Three it is, Sidlow."

Cursing at the dealer, Sidlow scooped his cards off the table.

When they all had their cards and everyone had opened but Meade, Meade looked over his cards, satisfied. He'd drawn an eight to a bobtail straight queen down. Shoving some silver toward the small pile in the middle of the table, he said, "I'll bet the lim—"

Glimpsing a shadow sliding over his left shoulder, Meade felt his heart leap. Adrenaline surging, he clawed his revolver from its holster and twisted around, dropping his left foot from the railing and rising awkwardly on his right leg. A dark figure stood behind him, silhouetted in the moonlight. The man wore a dark frock and a flat-brimmed black hat.

Hawk.

Meade thumbed his Remington's hammer back and squeezed the trigger. The Remy leapt in his hand three times, the shots sounding like cannonballs in the close quarters, smoke billowing. He lost his footing and fell back against an adobe pillar, firing two more times as he slid down the pillar, and once more when his butt hit the floor.

Sitting with his back to the pillar, his right leg bent, Meade blinked through the wafting powder smoke. The man he'd shot lay on the other side of the ramada, his head against the white adobe wall, liquid groans rising from his throat. The glass from shattered bottles covered the tiles around the groaning man's pajama-clad legs and rope-sandaled feet.

Meade's eyes narrowed and a muscle in his right cheek quivered. What the hell? Not Hawk, after all?

To Meade's left, the other poker players sat where they'd been sitting before the shooting, all staring slack-jawed toward the man on the far side of the ramada.

"Jesus Christ," one of them said in a hushed voice, "he shot John-John."

The dealer stood slowly, sliding his chair back, and moved slowly toward the injured man.

Meade blinked and looked around, disoriented. He looked at the man he'd shot. A short, stocky gent, he could see now. Round, pale face with a wispy mustache and slanted eyes. The man wore a black smock. Meade looked around the man's twisted body. No hat anywhere. Just a lot of broken glass winking in the moonlight.

Shit. He could have sworn the man was wearing a flat-brimmed black hat like Gideon Hawk's.

Meade's heart slowed a little, his anxiety replaced with embarrassment. The son of a bitch sure as hell *looked* like Hawk.

"Who the hell is John-John?" Meade croaked, getting his right leg and his hands under his butt, beginning to push himself up off the floor. "And what the hell was he doin', sneakin' up behind me like.that?"

"Cook's helper," said one of the men at the table. "Tended the garden and cleaned up around the place. He was gatherin' up whiskey bottles so the cook could refill 'em from his still."

Alarmed voices drifted down from the second story and from the main gate, the guards moving toward the hacienda to see what the shooting had been about.

"It's all right," the player called Sidlow yelled to the others, drifting toward the wounded man, still holding his cards in his hands. "Meade . . . uh, *Mister* Meade . . . shot John-John."

"What the hell did he do that for?" asked one of the guards standing out in the moonlit yard, chuckling.

"Ask him," said the dealer, crouched over John-John.

"Anyone sneaks up behind me, they better be ready for a pill they can't digest," Meade snarled, trying to quell the shaking in his hands as he ran a puffy silk shirtsleeve across his sweating forehead.

Sidlow and the dealer crouched over the groaning Chinaman for a few seconds. The wounded man rattled off some inexplicable phrases, kicked a leg, and sighed.

"He's had it," Sidlow said, shaking his head and drawing his pistol. "Best put him down." He and the dealer stepped back as Sidlow drew his pistol, extended the gun at the Chinaman's head, thumbed back the hammer, and pulled the trigger.

The gun popped, its flash lighting up the whole ramada. The Chinaman's head sagged to his right shoulder, and the shoulder sagged to the floor.

"This is really gonna piss-burn the cook," said one of the men sitting at the table.

"Fuck the cook," Meade growled, scooping his silver off the table and dropping it into a small, leather pouch. "I'm turnin' in."

He grabbed his crutches from where they'd been leaning against the sagging oak rail. Cursing, he hobbled into the hacienda, where the squeals of whores rose from the rooms and corridors around him and someone was absently strumming a guitar. He'd just turned through a broad, arched doorway when a figure appeared ahead of him, standing atop a four-step rise. The woman had long, wheat-yellow hair coiled in a tall bun atop her head, and a heart-shaped face. She was tall and thin, but her hard eyes, perpetually glassy from drink, kept her from being pretty.

Nice figure, though, which she showed off in a low-cut, wasp-waisted, lime-green dress with pleated skirts.

"Evening, Miss Ivy," Meade said with a courtly dip of his head as he leaned on his crutches.

She held a short, brown cigar to her lips, inhaled deeply. "What was the shooting about?" she asked with no real interest, blowing a thin stream of smoke toward the rafters.

"I shot a Chinaman named John-John."

"Oh. He spies on me while I'm bathing."

"He *spied* on you," Meade corrected, pushing off his right foot and swinging out the left crutch, moving toward the steps. He stopped and gazed up at her, running his eyes over her lush figure, her breasts pushing up from her corset like two big scoops of ice cream. "I bet he got an eyeful."

She cocked her head and curled a lip, her blue-green eyes twinkling. "He *did*."

"Your man working late tonight?"

"Doesn't he always?"

In a distant part of the hacienda, a man cut loose with an uproarious laugh. Meade carefully negotiated the steps with his crutches, peered down at the woman lustfully. "Care for a nightcap?"

She gave him a sidelong, up-and-down look. "Your cousin has provided plenty of whores for his men, which I know you're well aware of. Would you like me to summon one for you?"

"Nah," Meade said, grinning. "You'll do just fine."

Her eyes sharpened suddenly. She drew her arm back and forward, her hand connecting soundly with his face. Meade's head jerked to one side. His loins tingled, the slap's burn like kerosene thrown on a flame. His lust blazed.

Contrary to what Ivy thought, he hadn't slept with his cousin's whores. He'd slipped his hand down a dress now and then, but disease horrified him, and he didn't like the syphilitic look of Dayton's girls, most imported from Nogales.

Ivy held out her hand, palm up. He arched a puzzled brow.

"Your key," she said, her brows furrowed, hard eyes lowered to her hand. "I was going to wait in your room, but your door was locked."

Meade studied her. How impolite—bedding your cousin's woman. Especially after all that Dayton had done for Meade, getting him out of that mess up in Yank-

ton. What the hell? Ned had just been playing around—
it was *her* idea.

"Hurry up—Dayton could be back anytime," she
snapped.

Hot with the prospect of bedding this tough little mus-
tang—some prospector's or dirt farmer's daughter, no
doubt—Meade dug his key from his trouser pocket and
set it in her hand. She wheeled, her sandals clacking on
the tiles as she disappeared down the murky corridor lit
by occasional tapers.

Meade hobbled along behind her, turning left along a
courtyard in which a dry fountain stood amidst several
crumbling rock benches and next to a dead pecan tree
limned by moonlight. His room opened off the corridor.
The iron-banded door stood wide. Turning through it, he
paused just inside to watch her pouring whiskey at the
table by his bed, her back to him.

As she threw the drink back, he hoisted himself forward, then nudged the door closed with a crutch.

"To what do I owe the honor?" Meade asked. He
wasn't flush right now, and he wasn't fool enough to believe that any woman had ever slept with him for his
looks.

She set the glass on the table, turned to him, and
peeled the dress off her shoulders, squirming alluringly
as she slid it down her arms. "A bullet made him impo-
tent. Told me *after* he'd run my husband out of town."

The breasts—long and full, the brown nipples hard
and erect—bobbed free as the dress fell to her waist. She
sat on the bed, bare from the waist up, and unpinned her
hair, letting the coils fall down around her shoulders. She

glanced at him standing before the door, propped on his crutches.

"It doesn't run in the family, does it?"

Chuckling, Meade stuck his key in the lock, then maneuvered over to the bed, plopped down beside her, tossed his crutches against a nearby chair, and began unbuttoning his shirt. She wasn't wearing underwear, so she was as naked as the day she was born before Meade had finished with his shirt.

Kneeling, she pulled his right boot off, then helped peel his underwear down his leg.

"Christ, I've never fucked a man with a broken leg before."

"It's only my leg that's broken." She fell against the cast. "Ouch easy!"

"Oh, for Christ's sake!" She tossed his wash-worn underwear bottoms onto the chair, then slipped under the bedcovers. "Are you always that pale?"

As she straddled him, he took her full breasts in his hands, squeezing and fingering the nipples, trying to summon the arousal he'd been in before she'd nearly cracked his cast in her exuberance to get him undressed.

"Come on, come on," she urged, propped on one arm as she stroked his member with her other hand.

When she'd gotten him inside her, she gave two thrusts, then stopped and stared down at him smokily, her hair brushing his chest. "When you kill Dayton, take me with you to Mexico?"

He blinked up at her, not quite sure she'd said what he thought she'd said.

"I heard you and Patterson talking," she explained, a cunning light showing behind the lust in her eyes. She gave her hips another, single thrust. "Take me to Mexico, and you'll never want for nights like this."

"Why?" he grunted, her hips gripping him.

She scowled. "I was with a drunken, small-town sheriff for six years, then a man who couldn't get it up." The woman's eyes flashed. "I want excitement and money!"

Meade shrugged, opened and closed his hands on her thighs. "How could I say no?"

When they'd finished and she'd slipped furtively out of his room, he lulled himself to sleep by imagining how—after his dear cousin was dead and he'd taken the man's men and money—he'd kill her.

16.

BONNIE SPRINGS

HAWK and Joe DeRosso dumped the bodies of the two dead deputies in a shallow ravine, then slept until dawn. Backtracking the deputies to their camp on the south side of a pine-clad mountain slope, they turned the lawmen's Mexican prisoner loose with the deputies' horses, and continued southwest.

They descended the mountains into high desert country near the Mexican border, the pines giving way to chaparral, with now and then a roadrunner or javelina crossing their path. The sun was a brassy ball, the light intense, but this late in the year the heat was only mildly uncomfortable.

"Bonnie Springs dead ahead," DeRosso said at midday, reining his dun to a halt and sleeving sweat from his brow.

Hawk halted the pinto left of the former sheriff and peered into the valley through which the wide, flat Rio Grande snaked. Along the cactus-studded, rock-stippled slopes on the river's north side lay a good-sized town, stone and log shops and private dwellings built around the square of an old adobe pueblo. A brown adobe church abutted the square's west end, fronted by a dry fountain. Even farther west stood a smelter spewing thick, black smoke.

"Tell me about this place," Hawk said when he'd taken a drink from his canteen and looped it back over his saddle horn.

"What's to describe?" DeRosso grumbled, staring coldly into the valley, where the bulk of the movement was made up of heavy ore wagons dropping into the valley from the Mexican side of the river and grinding along the trail toward the smelter. "It's a town run by outlaws, but the inhabitants don't care. For all Priest's squawk and wattle, he keeps the outlaws away from the mine, and protects the shipments to Tucson. I coulda done that, too, if the mining company would have supplemented my income like they do Priest's. And hired me as many 'deputies.'"

"Why didn't they?"

"The mine was new. And small. I only had three deputies, and we was overrun. All this you see here—all these wagons, that smelter and stamping mill, hell, they only been here the past few months." DeRosso rolled a matchstick around between his lips, scowling down at the town. "Hell, they'll all be gone in another six months, and this place'll be a ghost town. Priest'll take his money and live high on the hog in Mexico." He gave the matchstick another roll. "Wonder if he's still got Ivy, or tired of her and put her up in one of his whorehouses?"

"You want her back?"

"Hell, no. I want her to see me raise some hell."

"Well," Hawk said, touching spurs to his paint's ribs, "let's go down and raise some hell."

"Now?" DeRosso said, surprised. "I thought we'd hole up on the ridge and wait till dark."

Hawk looked back over his right shoulder. "Why would we do that?"

"Hell, they'll recognize me. They'll probably recognize you, too. You don't think they won't be expectin' you, do you?"

Hawk turned his gaze back over his horse's bobbing head. "We wouldn't want to disappoint them, now, would we, Joe?"

"Shit," the ex-sheriff said, gigging his horse along behind Hawk, eyes hooded darkly. When he'd saved Hawk's life by shooting the two deputies, Hawk had rescinded his refusal to let him ride along with him to Bonnie Springs. Now, DeRosso was starting to wonder if he shouldn't have gone on back to the saloon.

"Marshal," he said behind Hawk, "you haven't gone a little out of your head, have you?"

"Me?" Hawk said. "Nah."

They rode down into the town, and Hawk turned his horse up to the large white adobe that had once been the Banco Nacional, but was now the sheriff's office. Four horses were tied to the hitch rack—tall, big-boned, well-groomed mounts tossing their heads haughtily. Obviously, these horses weren't used to sharing their hitch rack with strangers.

DeRosso's heart raced as Hawk tied his paint to the rack. "Hawk!" he hissed, shuttling his exasperated gaze between the marshal and the building's dust-streaked front windows. "What in God's name—?"

"Sit tight," Hawk said. "I might need a hand in a minute."

Hawk shucked his Henry from his saddle boot, stepped onto the cobbled walk before the office, knocked twice on the heavy timbered door, and stepped inside. The building's interior was cool and dark. There were gun racks and land-office plats where the tellers' cages once had been. Behind the rail separating the bank's small lobby from the office area were several desks. One man in a long, black duster and wearing a crisp sugar-loaf sombrero sat behind one of the desks, polished black boots crossed on the desktop. Two other men, also wearing dusters, gathered around him, stone coffee mugs in their hands. They looked like churchgoers talking after a Sunday service. They were big. Hawk didn't think any of the trio was under six-three.

They turned owly looks at the newcomer. Last night, chatting while they were dumping the deputies in the ravine, DeRosso had given Hawk a description of Priest. None of these three looked like him. Besides, their belligerent, flat-eyed faces owned a lackey flavor.

"Where's Priest?" Hawk said, holding his rifle low in his right hand.

The looks grew owlier. The two men sitting on the railing, their backs to him, stood and turned toward him, automatically taking their coffee cups in their left hands and sweeping their dusters back from the pistols on their right hips. One sported a short belly gun as well.

"Who the fuck's askin'?" said the one at the desk. "And it's *Sheriff* Priest."

"When you find him, tell him someone's waitin' for him over at the Tres Toros across the street."

Hawk turned and walked out, closing the door behind him. On the other side, one of the deputies bellowed, "Who's *someone*?"

Hawk stepped off the boardwalk and slipped his reins off the rack. Sitting the dun partway out in the street, DeRosso watched him warily, sweating like a trail cook, the sheriff's rifle in his hand. "Let's wet our whistles," Hawk said, swinging up into the hurricane deck.

DeRosso's sweaty face was drawn, his eyes sharp with anxiety. "That's the first smart thing I've heard from you all day!"

The office door clicked, and Hawk glanced over his shoulder. The deputy who'd been sitting behind the desk stepped onto the boardwalk, scowling. The other two flanked him. DeRosso turned sharply away, tipped his hat to hide his face, and followed Hawk to a hitch rack a half block away and on the other side of the street, before a saddle-and-gun shop.

When they'd tied their horses to the hitch rack fronted by a water trough, they loosened their saddle cinches, and DeRosso produced a Colt .38 from his saddlebags, checking to make sure the second gun was loaded before shoving it behind his cartridge belt, over his belly.

He and Hawk mounted the boardwalk, heading back up the street, toward the low adobe saloon sitting alone on a lot choked with buckbrush and Spanish bayonet. Hawk glanced at the sheriff's office. All three men stood on the boardwalk in the shade beneath the awning, watching him.

Inside the dusky saloon, seven or eight miners—Mex-

ican and American—were drinking in oafish silence.
None played cards or even chatted. They sat singly or in
pairs, one man standing at the pine bar, carving his ini-
tials into the ancient bar top that was a grid of old knife
gouges.

In a back room, a man strummed a guitar and sang
softly in Spanish, maybe practicing for an evening per-
formance. The strumming was accompanied by the dis-
parate sounds of rough lovemaking upstairs—squeaking
bedsprings, a girl complaining in throaty Spanish, and a
man dully retorting, "Shut up," after each squeak and
thud of the headboard striking the wall.

When Hawk and DeRosso had each ordered double
shots of the local *aguardiente,* the only thing the
grotesquely fat Mexican barman was serving, they sat
down at one of the square, pine-plank tables in the shadows at the back of the room. DeRosso was fidgety, glancing around at the other drinkers to see if any recognized
him. Apparently, none did, and he relaxed slightly as he
sat across from Hawk and threw back his drink.

"So, where is this going?" DeRosso asked.

"I thought he had twenty or so deputies."

"They must be out guarding an ore shipment to Tucson or Prescott. Or they might be off robbing Mexican
trains. It's a hobby of theirs."

Hawk stuck his tongue into the whiskey, tasting it.
"There's gotta be more than just those three deputies."

"Oh, there is. They're around." DeRosso studied him.
His voice was brittle with nerves. "Were you really just
going to walk into the sheriff's office and *shoot* Priest,
just like that?"

Hawk sipped the drink. "No. I was going to walk into

the office, tell him who I am and why I was there, and *then* I was going to shoot him."

DeRosso laughed dryly, made a conscious effort to keep his voice down. "*Then* what the hell were you going to do?"

"Ride out to Priest's hacienda and shoot Meade."

The laughter drained out of DeRosso's haggard features. Keeping his eyes on Hawk, he threw back the rest of his drink and set the empty glass on the table. "You wanna die, don't you?"

Hawk didn't say anything.

"Listen, my friend, I might be a one-handed drunk, but I kinda figure someday I'm gonna pick up the pieces again, you know? Make a life for myself. I'd kinda like to stick around to do it."

"All you have to do is back my play," Hawk said. "I'll make all the first moves. When the dust settles, you can get the local photographer to take a picture of you with your wife and Priest's carcass, and autograph it for her. Fair enough?"

DeRosso stared at him, his eyes moving around slightly. He chuckled dryly, whistling softly through his teeth, and drew his pistol. He opened the loading gate and filled the empty chamber beneath the hammer, gave the cylinder a spin, then returned the piece to its holster. He tapped his boots on the floor.

Hawk reached across the table, grabbed his right wrist, sliding back the duster sleeve to reveal the red stump resembling the end of a hastily wrapped sausage cylinder.

His boots falling silent, DeRosso looked at Hawk's hand on his wrist, then at Hawk's face. The man's eyes bored into his. "How'd they do it?" Hawk asked.

DeRosso stared back at him, tried to pull his arm away, but Hawk held it fast. DeRosso lowered his gaze to Hawk's gloved hand squeezing his wrist just up from the stump.

"Priest and four of his thugs, including one of the men we just saw across the street, sauntered into my office one day and told me he was taking over and that my wife had moved out to his hacienda. Priest shot one of my deputies without warning, point-blank range, then turned the gun on me.

"My two other deputies turned in their badges, and I went to a saloon. The next night, dog-faced drunk, I went back to the office and raised hell, even squeezed off a couple rounds. Priest's deputies wrestled me down, dragged me out back to the block where an old Mex woman butchered her chickens."

DeRosso swallowed hard, tightened his lips across his teeth. "They held a big bowie to my throat and told me it was my gun hand or my balls—my decision. I quit fighting and draped my arm across that chopping block, and they chopped off my hand with that blood-crusty old hatchet."

DeRosso's lips quivered, and a tear dribbled down from each eye. His face flushed with fury.

Hawk released the man's wrist, a satisfied cast in his gaze, and threw back the last of his drink. He and DeRosso stared out the window for a few minutes. The three deputies from the saloon appeared on the other side of the street. Another man had joined them—just as tall but older, with long, stringy black hair and burnsides. He wore a long, black duster with a sheriff's badge pinned to the lapel, and a crisp, gray sombrero with a smooth leather band around the crown. The four waited for a string of mule-drawn freight wagons to pass, then crossed the street, angling toward the cantina's front door. They were all carrying rifles down low at their sides, their expressions grave.

Hawk removed his rifle from the tabletop and quietly levered a round into the chamber. "Ready to dance?"

17.

DANCE

T HE man with the sheriff's star stood peering over the batwings, his tall, bulky frame silhouetted by the bright light behind him. After a few seconds, he pushed through the doors and stepped into the room, stopped again, and stood gawking around as the three deputies flanked him.

"Who wants to see me?" His voice wasn't deep or resonant for a big man. It was even a little high and raspy, as though he'd once screamed too loud and injured it.

"That's him back there," said the deputy on his right, the same man who'd been sitting behind the desk in the sheriff's office.

Priest squinted into the shadows, his lips parted so that his mouth made a dark oval as he raked air in and out of his lungs. His eyes were dark and his hawkish nose worked like a dog's.

He tipped his head back. "You wanna see me?" He barely got the last two words out, for his gaze had moved to DeRosso sitting to Hawk's right. He froze. Then his lips came together and rose slightly at the corners. "Well, look who's home."

Priest took two slow steps forward, the deputies moving in beside him, one on his right, two on his left. The four men between the lawmen and Hawk and DeRosso weren't between them long. Taking their drinks, three scurried over to the bar. One scurried to the opposite wall. Then, deciding that wasn't where he wanted to be, he bolted across the room and out the front door, the batwings shuddering behind him.

Upstairs, the springs had stopped squeaking, and the girl was berating the man quietly in Spanish, barely audible through the ceiling and above the rattle of occasional freight outfits on the street. The fat bartender sat his stool behind the bar, staring toward the lawmen, his small eyes wary, jaws sagging, the folds of his face and neck hanging toward his chest.

"I told you if you came back I'd kill you," Priest told DeRosso.

DeRosso didn't say anything.

"Who's your friend?" Priest asked, returning his gaze to Hawk.

DeRosso canted a glance at his partner. "Mind if I introduce you?"

"Why not?" Hawk said, sitting back in his chair as though waiting for a sermon to begin. His lips shaped a faint smile, but his eyes were as dark as a cold October night.

"Dayton Priest, meet Gideon Hawk." DeRosso squeezed the words with exaggerated politeness through gritted teeth.

As he stared at Hawk, Priest's eyes flattened, like a lamp extinguished in the depths of a deep cave. The right eye twitched slightly. So gradually as to barely be noticeable, the heavy forehead seemed to bulge out over Priest's eyes, bunching the bridge of his nose. For a time, his whole body was still as stone.

Around him, the deputies fidgeted, their sneers replaced with edgy frowns. They seemed to be fighting with themselves to keep their rifles down.

"You're Ned's friend," Priest said, his eyes boring into Hawk's.

"I ran into Marshal Hawk back in Paris," DeRosso said. "I figure he's as good as my right hand." Hawk saw him grin out of the corner of his vision. "Maybe a tad better."

Without moving anything but his mouth, Priest said, "Didn't happen to run into two of my deputies up that way, did you?"

DeRosso grinned again. "Uh-huh."

The deputy to Priest's right chuffed faintly with anger, his right cheek bunching, his right hand squeezing his rifle around the forestock.

Priest's eyes flicked to DeRosso. Hawk followed them. DeRosso sat straight in his chair, both hands beneath the table. Behind the lawmen, two miners entered the saloon, gabbing loudly. Spying the to-do at the back of the saloon, they stopped talking, turned around, and hustled back out through the doors.

Flicking his gaze around, Hawk saw that the other drinkers had left as well. The barman must be crouched behind the bar, for Hawk hadn't seen the fat man leave.

A fly buzzed around Priest's face. The sheriff wrinkled

his nose, and the fly landed on the badge pinned to his lapel.

In a blur, Priest snapped his rifle up. Hawk followed suit, swinging his Henry out from beneath the table and squeezing the trigger.

The shot sounded like a powder keg exploding in the close quarters. Hawk's slug drilled Priest's star and, sparks flying, slammed the sheriff straight back onto the hard-packed earthen floor with a guttural cry. Priest's rifle discharged into the rafters, dust sifting.

Everything moved very slowly after that, Hawk seeing DeRosso leaping to his feet, his chair flying back as he extended his six-shooter at the deputy closest him, and firing, the revolver roaring and leaping in his hand. At the same time, Hawk swung his Henry left, drilling the second deputy through the neck, ramming another round into his chamber, and bearing down on the deputy farthest out.

The man fired a half second before Hawk did, the slug burning along the surface of Hawk's neck.

As the deputy levered another shell, he flung himself toward the bar, and Hawk's round plunked into a joist, shattering an unlit lantern. Kneeling behind a chair, the deputy extended his rifle over the chair's right arm and fired, the bullet taking Hawk across the right upper arm.

Hawk swung toward the man. In the corner of his right eye, he saw a gun flash, felt a slug part his hair at the back of his head as the man who'd pulled the trigger flung himself out the front window with a deafening thunder of shattering glass.

Hawk raised his Henry as the deputy jacked a fresh round and lowered the barrel. Hawk fired. At the same time, DeRosso triggered his pistol to his right and behind him. Both slugs punched through the chair back, two inches apart, and into the deputy's forehead, ramming the man back against the bar, his back taut, his mouth opening and closing as he died.

The twin holes looked like a second pair of eyes until the blood appeared, glistening in the wan light penetrating the shadows from the room's front window.

Hawk ejected the spent shell, levered fresh, and raised the rifle again to his shoulder, swinging right, the barrel tracking the room with his eyes. All three deputies were down. DeRosso stood ten feet away, his smoking pistol extended in his left hand. He and Hawk shared a brief glance, then shuttled their gazes to the broken front window.

"In there!" someone shouted from outside. "Get those son o' *bitches*!"

Hawk and DeRosso ran to the batwings and, standing side by side, looked out.

His face and hands bloody from small glass cuts, and clutching his bloody chest around the tin star on his lapel, Priest lay on his right hip in the street, left of the saloon and at the intersection of a cross street.

Hatless, he looked back at the saloon. Four men, all wearing black or brown dusters, twill trousers stuffed into high-topped boots, and five-pointed stars, jogged toward the saloon from the west. All were equally dust-caked, their faces glistening with sweat, as if they'd just returned from a long trail ride.

Traffic on the street had stopped, and the boardwalks were vacated.

"The cantina!" Priest bellowed tightly, clutching his

chest, his black hair catching in the blood smeared about his forehead and cheeks.

The four deputies, brows furrowed under their broad hat brims, raised their Henrys, barrels up, as they jogged past the sheriff and approached the saloon at an angle.

"You take the two on the right," Hawk told DeRosso, thumbing fresh shells into his Henry's loading tube. "I'll take the two on the left."

"Who gets Priest?"

"First come, first served."

"Fair enough," DeRosso muttered, pushing through the batwings, leaping off the boardwalk, and running out between two horses tethered to the hitch rack.

At the same time, Hawk stepped onto the boardwalk, pressed his back against the cantina's front wall, and raised his Henry to his shoulder.

"There!" one of the deputies shouted, stopping forty feet away and bringing his rifle to bear. He didn't get the gun to his shoulder before Hawk drilled him through the belly.

As the belly-shot deputy folded up like a pocketknife, DeRosso ran out from behind the horses and opened up with his pistol. Hawk ducked two shots, then cut down another deputy with three quick shots, hastily aiming but spinning the man around and down just the same.

As DeRosso emptied his first pistol and snapped off two shots with the second, clipping the legs out from a deputy bolting toward a water trough on the other side of the street, Hawk stepped off the boardwalk, set his rifle against the hitch rack, and unholstered his Colt. Three deputies were down and still, limbs akimbo, bloody dusters fanned out around them like giant birds fallen from the sky.

DeRosso strode toward the deputy who'd fallen before the stock trough. The man was climbing to one knee and reaching for his rifle lying in horse plop.

DeRosso stopped three feet away from the man, extended his pocket pistol straight out from his shoulder, and drilled a .38 slug through the man's face. The man snapped back with a two-syllable grunt, legs jerking wildly before relaxing, one after the other.

Meanwhile, Priest lay about twenty yards away, at the cross street's intersection with the main drag. He'd crawled a few yards from his former position, leaving a bloody dirt swath in the street behind his polished boots with their glistening, large-roweled spurs.

He had a .45 in his right hand, but the arm was wedged beneath his body. He grunted and scowled, trying to raise the gun while cupping his left hand to his chest, trying to stop the blood. It didn't work, and he gave up, letting the long-barreled Colt sag in the dirt.

Side by side, Hawk and DeRosso stood over him, looking down, their expressions at once grave and repelled. Priest looked around the street, eyes wide, jaws sagging, as if seeking help from the citizens. They all stayed locked within their businesses, ghostly faces gazing through dusty windows.

"He's yours," Hawk said.

"Nah," DeRosso said. "You can have him."

Staring down at Priest, Hawk said, "He took your hand. You deserve him."

"He freed the man who killed your boy," DeRosso countered.

Priest stared up at them through hooded, pleading eyes, lips moving as he muttered incoherently.

"I know," Hawk said. "Let's both take him."

Both men extended their pistols, thumbed back the hammers, and squeezed the triggers.

Ned Meade stood on the balcony of his room at Priest's "ranch," crutches propped beneath his arms. He wore nothing but a black silk night jacket with a Chinese folk symbol gold-stitched on the right breast. The unbuttoned jacket hung straight down from his shoulders. He puffed a thick stogie while holding a half-filled sherry glass in his other hand.

"What the hell is all that shooting about?" he groused, staring westward toward Bonnie Springs. The town lay two miles away, but low, chalky hills impeded his view. Another two pistol shots rose, sounding like little more than firecrackers from this distance, but they came on the heels of a veritable fusillade.

"Maybe someone's trying a bank robbery," said the bare-breasted woman on the bed behind him, absently brushing her hair. She chuckled huskily. "Or maybe they're trying to make off with one of the ore wagons again."

Nervously, Meade puffed the stogie and stared at the hills.

"Don't worry," Ivy DeRosso said. "Dayton has plenty of deputies."

Meade chewed the stogie and loosed another smoke puff. "He's got eight men in Mexico till the end of the week," he growled, as much to himself as to her.

He lowered his gaze from the scrubby hills turning

green as the sun slanted westward. Priest had left five men at the hacienda, and they all stood inside the six-foot adobe wall surrounding the sprawling house, staring through the open wooden gate.

Meade removed the cigar from between his teeth and yelled, "I've got a novel idea! Instead of standing around with your thumbs up your asses, why don't one of you get the hell out there and find out what all the shooting's about?"

Two men turned toward him. "We're all s'posed to stay with the house," one of them said, wearing fringed hide breeches and wielding a double-barreled shotgun.

"You're takin' orders from me now," Meade shot back. *"Pronto!"*

The man who'd spoken turned to the others and shrugged. One jogged out the gate, reappearing a few minutes later on a saddled horse trotting down the curving drive to the main trail. He cantered up the chalky ridge, his shadow long behind him, and disappeared down the other side.

Meade had hobbled back into the bedroom and was pouring himself a fresh drink when another flurry of gunshots rose from the other side of the hill.

18

SPECIAL DELIVERY

A T the sound of the shots, Meade jerked with a start, smashing the brandy decanter against his glass, knocking it over and spilling brandy across his dresser. He dropped the glass stopper and whipped his head toward the open balcony doors. "What the hell was *that*?"

The woman didn't say anything. She stopped brushing her hair and absently drew her sheer lemon-yellow wrapper across her breasts. Meade moved passed her, stumbling over his boots, and hobbled back onto the balcony.

Below, the four men stood abreast at the open gate, staring west.

Two more shots sounded, followed by a third. They sounded considerably closer than the others, somewhere between the low hills and the town.

The deputies looked at each other. One scratched the back of his head, nudging his hat up.

"What the hell was that?" Meade shouted. His heart

was pounding, and he felt as though an iron band were squeezing his head.

One of the men looked back at him, his disdain apparent even from this distance. "More shootin'." He grunted, jerking his head slightly, and returned his gaze westward.

"More shootin'," Meade mocked, rolling the cigar from one side of his mouth to the other.

He stood there, gazing at the pale, two-track trail curving up the purpling hills, until his leg got tired. He sat down in a wicker chair, propping the crutches against the wall behind him. He sat sipping the brandy, puffing the cigar, lighting another, and trying to quell his nerves.

It couldn't be Hawk. The man could not have found him here. . . .

The sun set in a golden-ochre wash, and the first stars kindled in the violet sky above the hacienda. The deputies had lit torches and mounted them here and there about the courtyard, casting shadows across the scuffed grounds before the gates.

"Wagon comin' in a hurry!" one of the men shouted from the other side of the wall.

Meade frowned, listening. The thunder and rattle of steel-shod wheels slowly rose to his ears. He reached for the crutches, hoisted himself up from the chair. "What in Christ's name is going on?"

He turned to the lantern-lit room behind him, where the woman lay across the bed, reading a magazine, her hair thrown over one shoulder. She'd donned a poncho against the evening chill, but little else.

"I'm going down there," he said. "Give me a hand!"

When the woman had helped him through the arched passageways and down several sets of steps to the courtyard, Meade could feel the ground shuddering beneath his feet. The wagon's clatter sounded like rushing thunder.

Standing at the bottom of the last set of steps, he grabbed his crutch from the woman, planted it under his arm, and leaned into it. He was about to swing the right crutch forward when, shuttling his gaze left to the open gate forty yards away, he froze.

Two sets of eyes blazed in the darkness between the gates, causing Meade's breath to catch in his throat. A fraction of a second later, the heads and bodies of the mules emerged from the night, drawing the screeching, hammering hay wagon on through the gate, turning a broad semicircle far left of Meade before halting suddenly by a low, rock wall dividing the main grounds from a trio of dead lemon trees.

Both mules lowered their heads and brayed raucously, shaking their heavy collars.

The driver's box was empty, the reins tied loosely to the brake.

The deputies had stood wide of the gate, watching the wagon lumber into the yard, their rifles raised to their shoulders, hammers cocked back. Now they rose and slowly converged on the wagon from its right side, keeping their rifles raised, the hammers cocked.

While two looked over the side of the wagon box, two swung around to the back, their rifles canted downward. From his position, Meade could see little but hay or straw piled in the box, an oblong figure lying in the middle of it.

When the deputies lowered their rifles and muttered to each other, casting cautious glances around the yard and the open gate, Meade hobbled into the courtyard, angling toward the wagon. The deputies made way for him. He stood at the end of the box, peering inside.

His cousin, Dayton Priest, lay atop the hay, his bloody body spread-eagle, glassy eyes reflecting the vagrant torchlight as they stared unseeing at the stars. Under his sheriff's badge lay a large scrap of blood-stained paper upon which words had been scrawled in block letters.

Meade ripped the paper from under the badge, held it to his face, canting it slightly to catch the wavering, umber light.

"Special Delivery," he read aloud. "To Ned Meade in care of Priest's whore."

Meade lowered the paper and turned slowly, a shudder running through him.

"He's found me," he whispered to himself, running his eyes along the adobe wall separating the hacienda's grounds from the dark night beyond. "I'll be damned . . . he found me. . . ."

"I've come to buck the tiger, Ned." The voice had come from behind him.

Meade stiffened. He and the deputies had all been facing the grounds. Now, slowly, all at the same time, they turned back to the wagon and peered into the box. Only Priest was there, his sightless eyes and bloody badge reflecting the shuddering torchlight.

In the hay behind the body, something moved. The light flickered off a pistol barrel protruding from the hay. Another soft rustle, and another barrel appeared two feet right of the first.

"Hey!" one of the deputies yelled, jerking his rifle up.

He didn't get it halfway to his shoulder before both pistols stabbed smoke and fire, lighting up the inside of the wagon. The deputy staggered back, and then another went down, and another dropped near Meade's right crutch. The shooting continued as Meade, shocked and disoriented, staggered backward, wincing with each shot and at the yells and screams of the dying deputies.

Meade clawed at the grips of the pistol on his right hip, got the gun caught in his crutch, and went down with a groan, hitting the ground hard on his left shoulder and leg.

Hawk was crouched beside Priest's body, hay clinging to his coat and hat and to the revolver extended before him. DeRosso had emerged from the pile at the same time as Hawk, and he knelt to Hawk's left, peering over the left side of the wagon.

Their gun smoke hung around them like a fetid fog.

After raking his gaze around Priest's deputies, lying in twisted piles around the wagon, Hawk turned his eyes to Meade, sighing and grunting on the ground ten yards off the end of the wagon.

Hawk leapt down from the wagon box, took three quick strides, and kicked the gun out of Meade's hand just as Meade was thumbing back the hammer. The gun sailed twenty yards before hitting the ground with a clatter.

"Oh, Christ . . . I knew it was you," Meade rasped, pushing onto his elbows and heaving himself back a foot, then collapsing again with a grunt. "Please . . . I think I injured my leg again."

Hawk stood over him, gazing coldly down, saying nothing.

"All right, you have me," Meade said, stretching his

face back from his teeth painfully. "I can't go anywhere. Fetch me a horse, and I'll come peaceably."

Hawk heard footsteps on his left, and turned to DeRosso walking up beside him. "Bring the wagon," Hawk said.

Hawk crouched over Ned, whose eyes snapped wide with fear. "What are you doin'?" Ned cried.

Hawk grabbed a handful of the man's long hair, jerked Meade off his butt, and began dragging him across the grounds. Meade screamed and clawed at Hawk's hand, lifting his butt off the ground with his right leg to keep Hawk from ripping his scalp off. He twisted around, by turns grabbing at Hawk's fist and pushing off the ground, half-crawling, dragging his cast along behind.

As DeRosso turned the mules to follow Hawk, a dark figure caught his eye, and he turned toward the bottom of the steps. A woman sat huddled on the bottom step, holding a wrapper taut about her shoulders, in the shadows beneath the overarching lemon trees. Long blond hair fell over her right shoulder.

DeRosso turned away and continued leading the wagon after Hawk and the outlaw he was half-dragging by the man's bone-white hair.

Under the high, arched gateway, Hawk released Ned's hair, and the man fell with a groan, pressing his hands to his bleeding scalp. He turned an enraged gaze up at the man standing over him. "What the hell are you doing? I gave myself up! You have to take me back to Yankton for trial!"

Hawk pinched his trousers up his thighs and squatted down, cast his dark gaze at Meade. "You killed my boy, Ned."

"You killed my brother!"

"Your brother deserved to die. My boy did not."

"You have to take me in. I deserve a fair trial!"

"Not by my law."

Meade rose up on his right hip, twisting around at the hip and jabbing his dusty, sweat-streaked face at Hawk like a hatchet. "You're a marshal . . . you're a United States marshal, Hawk! You have to take me in!"

"You're gonna die slow, Ned. Real slow . . . so the devil has a good, long time to recognize your face."

The wagon rattled up behind Hawk. Meade turned to it, his eyes filling suddenly with the horrific realization of what was about to happen to him. Tears poured down his cheeks and his eyes glistened in the orange light shunting shadows about the yard.

Hawk turned. Eyes grave, DeRosso stood beside the mules and held out a coiled rope to Hawk, who took it and deftly fashioned a noose before Meade's terrified gaze.

"Please," Meade said, his shrill voice quaking. "I'm begging you now, Gideon."

As DeRosso turned the wagon around, Hawk walked around behind Meade, slipped the noose over the outlaw's neck, and yanked it tight.

Meade tried to dig the noose out from around his neck. "Oh, God, no!" he rasped.

Keeping the rope taut, Hawk tossed the coil over the gate's arch, about fifteen feet above the ground, then tied the end to an iron ferule on the wagon box. Priest's head had turned, and his dead eyes watched Hawk with awful fascination.

When Hawk had tied the knot, he turned to Meade.

The outlaw had gotten his fingers under the noose and was working it up toward his chin. Hawk grabbed the rope, snapped it tight. Meade's hands snapped down as the man fell face-forward, arms spread out on the ground, and made a garbled choking sound, still sobbing and pleading incoherently for his life.

Hawk released the rope, glanced at DeRosso standing at the head of the off mule, and nodded. Tugging on the mule's harness, DeRosso began walking forward.

Hawk turned to Meade. The man had quit fighting the noose, which had loosened enough that the outlaw could coherently plead for his life before the wagon drew the slack out of the rope, and again the noose slipped taut. Meade's head snapped toward the wagon, eyes narrowed from the pain.

The outlaw winced and puffed out his cheeks as his shoulders rose from the ground, his back straightening. DeRosso kept leading the wagon toward the house, and when he'd traveled twenty yards, the toes of Ned Meade's boots left the ground. A few seconds later, Meade was kicking, and clawing fruitlessly at the noose around his neck, his head only three feet from the bottom of the stone arch.

"That's far enough," Hawk said, raising his right hand.

Meade hacked and coughed, choking, furiously kicking with his good leg, turning in slow, jerky circles as if he could somehow shake free of the noose.

Hawk and DeRosso sat down at the end of the wagon, and watched Meade dance his death jig. It took a long time, and Hawk watched every second of it. In his mind's eye, he saw Jubal hanging from that big cottonwood atop the rain-lashed hill, his own lovely Linda hanging from the tree in their backyard.

As Meade's good leg ceased kicking, now only shaking beside the hard, white cast, his whole body convulsing intermittently, his eyes bulging from his skull, Hawk nodded. His family was avenged.

"Reckon we best get out of here, before any of Priest's 'deputies' return," DeRosso said.

Hawk didn't say anything. He kept his eyes on Meade's still form hanging under the arch. Again, he nodded dully. Climbing off the wagon, he headed for the driver's box. DeRosso followed suit, but stopped abruptly. The woman from the steps was moving toward him, like a ghost materializing from the flickering shadows.

Ivy looked up at him, her eyes large, tears streaking her cheeks. "Joe, you have no idea how relieved I am to see you."

"I got some idea," DeRosso growled.

"You don't know what it's been like, being here with"— her eyes strayed to the wagon box, where Priest gaped at them, a fly walking along his lower lip—"him."

DeRosso turned and walked to the end of the wagon. He grabbed Priest's left foot, and pulled the body out of the box, letting it drop to the ground with a hard thud. "I doubt it's gonna get much better." He turned back to the woman, frowning up at him. "But you have my blessing."

He pinched his hat brim and climbed up onto the wagon seat beside Hawk, who slapped the reins against the mules' backs, turning the wagon in a broad circle and heading back out through the gate, the men having to duck their heads under Meade's slowly turning boots.

The woman gaped behind them.

When they'd returned to their horses, which they'd tied to a stunted cottonwood in a dark creek bottom, they stepped off the wagon and released the mules from the hitch, slapping their rears and watching them head, braying, toward town.

"What're you gonna do now, Gideon?" DeRosso said as they reset their saddles on their horses' backs.

Hawk pressed his right fist against the paint's ribs, tightened the latigo, and cinched it. "I have some graves to visit up north. Then I reckon I'll head wherever the law takes me."

"Law?" DeRosso chuckled without humor. "What law?"

Hawk toed a stirrup and swung up into the leather. "My law." He reined the horse northward, stopped, and turned back to DeRosso staring up at him, the former sheriff's face a dark oval under his hat.

Hawk extended his left hand. "Luck to you, Joe."

"Luck to you, Gideon." DeRosso shook Hawk's hand, stepped back gravely as the rogue lawman touched spurs to his horse's ribs and galloped down the wash and into the night.

DeRosso stared after him. He pulled a bottle from his pocket, pulled the cork with his teeth, spat it out, and took a long pull.

Fifty yards away, Hawk reined his horse up out of the wash and pulled back on the reins. He looked around at the star-filled sky, glanced back at the orange glow of the hacienda's torches.

When he'd taken a reckoning on the stars, he tugged his hat low and lifted his collar against the chill. Reaching into a coat pocket, he pulled out his gloved hand and, holding it low against his thigh, opened it.

He ran his index finger over the wooden stallion's carefully scrolled mane and skyward-flailing hooves. He stared down at the figure. The horse swam through a teary blur.

Gideon raised the carving to his lips, then returned it to his pocket, shaking the wooden horse down deep so he wouldn't lose it.

He didn't have much left to lose.

He drew his collar closed at his throat, touched spurs to the paint's ribs, and headed north.

Peter Brandvold was born and raised in North Dakota. He currently resides in Colorado. Visit his website at www.peterbrandvold.com. Send him an E-mail at pgbrandvold@msn.com.